THOMAS TITANS
MEN AMONG BOYS

ADELINE FOO

OM
Om Books International

Adeline Foo completed her Master's of Fine Arts degree at New York University's Tisch School of the Arts on a Singapore Media Development Authority scholarship.

She has 21 published children's books, seven of which are national best-sellers. Adeline's *The Diary of Amos Lee* series is published in Singapore, India, Indonesia, China and now, the Slovak Republic. It has been adapted for a ten-part TV series on Singapore's MediaCorp children's channel, okto, and adopted as a secondary school English textbook for 13-year-olds.

One of her picture books, *Nu Nu, The Ring-Necked Monster*, is being developed into a children's play. Besides working on the screenplay for *Thomas Titans,* Adeline is also developing a game app *Are You A Dodo?* partnered with Singapore's most profitable gaming house. For author updates, please refer to www.adelinefoo.com

Thomas Titans Basketball League

"We're men among boys."

This edition first published in 2013 by

OM

Om Books International

Corporate & Editorial Office
A-12, Sector 64, Noida 201 301
Uttar Pradesh, India
Phone: +91 120 477 4100
Email: editorial@ombooks.com
Website: www.ombooksinternational.com

Sales Office
4379/4B, Prakash House, Ansari Road
Darya Ganj, New Delhi 110 002, India
Phone: +91 11 2326 3363, 2326 5303
Fax: +91 11 2327 8091
Email: sales@ombooks.com
Website: www.ombooks.com

ISBN: 978-93-82607-56-4

Printed in India

10 9 8 7 6 5 4 3 2 1

1
Introduction

I don't know who my father is. He disappeared when I was born. It took my mother twelve hours of labour – twelve hours of screaming – before she delivered me. She was only seventeen.

It has been a long time since my father left. I'm thirteen now. I still have no clue who he is. But I do know that my mother loved him very much.

—

Life without a father is tough. In a society where women usually get married before they have a baby, I get taunted a lot. I get called all kinds of ugly names. But I learnt very early on that I must never repeat to my mother what people said about me. She would only cry and hide in her room. As I grew older, I learnt to silence cruel tormentors in my own way.

In kindergarten, I was always made to clean out the pet cage. For some reason, teachers assumed that because I looked tough, I wouldn't be afraid to handle mice. Being the pet handler meant that I could devise ways to bully my tormentors in class.

There were at least twenty-one ways you could put mice to good use. My favourite prank was swaddling one with toilet paper and putting it in an unsuspecting person's bag. The terrified mouse would eventually gnaw its way out of the toilet paper and cause mayhem in the classroom. After a while, the kids around me realised that the pet handler was someone they shouldn't mess around with.

When I was about nine, I learnt that arm power could be put to good use too. It happened one day when I was at the playground with some kids. We were waiting to go down the slide. When it was my turn, a boy behind me yanked my shirt. He pushed me to the ground. When I struggled, he squashed my face in the sand. Then he laughed and yelled, "You don't belong here! Go away!"

When he got off my back, I picked myself up. I wiped the sand off my face and removed the sandal I was wearing. I waited till he was halfway down the slide, then I took aim. I threw the sandal with a strength I didn't even know I had. It hit him in the head. The boy yelped in pain. I went up to him and picked up my sandal. I looked at him fiercely. The boy looked scared when I said in a low voice, "Don't ever come near me again." He just nodded meekly.

That evening, the boy's mother came up to my flat. I heard her ranting about how badly my mother had brought me up. She even said I would end up in jail one day. My mother didn't say a word.

After the woman had gone off, my mother gave me a disappointed look and disappeared into her room. I wouldn't have minded a scolding. Or even a slap. But nothing. I went up to her door and put my ear to it. I heard her crying. Again.

I didn't start the fight; she didn't even ask.

I never saw the boy again. But I learnt his name from other kids. He was named after a prince. Edward, the third son of Queen Elizabeth II of England. The boy and his mother were visiting their relatives. I figured out as much; they looked too rich to be living in an estate of rental flats.

Over time, I gained a formidable reputation. Kids learnt to stay away from me. Just as well, as I had no need for friends. I worked hard to be better than everyone else, both in studies and sports. I never gave my teachers a reason to call my mother down to school. Who needed to, when Ayush Lee was the top boy in school and captain of the primary school basketball team?

2
Fight Club

It must have been the boredom of the holidays. The boys that I played basketball with came up with the idea of starting a Fight Club. One of them had seen the movie on YouTube and thought it would be fun to have a club for the boys. I wasn't really keen. But there was nothing better to do.

We set the ground rules. In Fight Club, the boys would engage in wrestling, with the objective of getting an opponent down on the ground. No kicking was allowed, and no below-the-belt punching. It was meant for workouts. Lots of thrusting and arm-blocking exercises. And mind work, too, in learning to trip your opponent.

I became the hero of Fight Club because I would win every fight. I was Brad Pitt to those scrawny, acne-ridden teenagers. It must have been my dark brown hair and sharp nose. Or maybe it was the cheekbones. Being born a Chindian – half Chinese and half Indian – makes me better looking than those Hokkien boys I played basketball with.

After a week of living in glory, things got out of hand. A street corner gang showed up. Somehow word had got out that we had started a new form of street fighting. When I saw the gangsters, I knew they were trouble. The gang members had bleached hair and identical tattoos. The leader wore a nose ring. They looked to be in their twenties!

When someone asked who the leader of Fight Club was, the boys looked at me uneasily. The leader – he called himself Shawn – challenged me to a fight. There, in front of ten boys, I couldn't back down.

Shawn approached me with a wild look in his eyes. He circled me cautiously and got excited when his friends cheered him on. I saw him take out a bunch of keys from his pocket. I ducked on instinct when he swung his fist at me. I missed it the first time.

But the second time his fist came around, I got hit in the cheek. I felt the sharp point of one of the keys. It stung. I touched my face and saw blood. I was angry. I looked at the others. They were shouting and punching their fists into the air. Their combined roar was deafening.

I stepped back, trying to see if there was something I could pick up to protect myself. Nothing. The next thing I knew, I felt a hard punch in my stomach. I bent over and felt vomit coming up my gut. I spat it out and wiped my mouth. I was mad and could feel my adrenalin rising. I body-slammed Shawn and grabbed his head in an arm lock. I bit his ear and forced him to drop his keys. I kicked the keys away and brought my knee up to his chest. Then I saw one of Shawn's friends coming towards me menacingly. I saw him flick open a penknife.

"No weapons!" I yelled.

Just when I thought the boy was going to knife me, I felt someone pull me from behind. It was an adult's strong pair of arms. I heard screaming, my mother's voice.

Screwed. Of all people, it had to be my mother who saved me.

She walked up to the boy holding the penknife and slapped him hard in the head. Then, in front of the other boys watching sheepishly, she pulled his left ear and twisted it hard.

"Ouch! Let me go! Okay, okay, I'm sorry!" he whined in pain.

My mother lashed out at the boys in a torrent of Hokkien words. She said she would call the police if they didn't leave. Everyone left, giving me a look of pity.

That night, I felt the strength of her anger. She caned me twenty times on the butt with a wooden rod. It was horribly painful, but nothing compared to the fate of being knifed at the basketball court.

I've often wondered how Mum can be both soft and fierce at the same time. Being called cruel names makes her cry. But when her son gets threatened, she turns into a Tiger Mum.

3
Fat Boy at the Basketball Court

My mother never mentioned the fight again. But every time I said I was playing basketball downstairs, she would give me *the look*.

I would just grin and say, "Yeah, yeah, no more Fight Club." She can be scary when she's dead serious.

One afternoon, I met a fat boy – a tall, bumbling idiot trying to do a three-point jump shot on the basketball court. He was trying so hard I felt sorry for him. His arms were short and pudgy. He just couldn't jump high enough. But he kept trying. I stood and counted. He must have tried at least eighteen times before the ball got in. I was happy for him, so I clapped.

Fat Boy heard me and turned around. He looked at me suspiciously. I shrugged and threw a pass at him with my ball. Fat Boy grabbed it deftly and started dribbling around me.

Another basketball maniac.

It was one-on-one. Fat Boy tried to get past me. He was looking for a clear shot at the basket. But my long arms and close guarding gave him no chance.

Then I heard a sweet voice call out, "Lasso!"

I stole a glance from the corner of my eye. Big mistake. Fat Boy drove past me and went straight for the basket to score an easy lay-up. I stared at him, aghast.

That was when The Vision appeared in front of me. She had a mass of cascading black hair. Her skin was smooth and clear. And her eyes, so soft and doe-like! My jaw dropped! This surely must be The World's Most Beautiful Girl!

The Vision swung her hair over her shoulders. I could smell sweet shampoo. I almost sighed. She turned to me and grinned.

"Hi," she said.

That same voice which had distracted me! Suddenly, I felt weak all over. I couldn't utter a word.

"Come on, let's go!" The girl was now wheedling at Fat Boy. He threw my ball back at me. I caught it and nodded my thanks.

Fat Boy had a beautiful girlfriend, I thought to myself. I was jealous. And he was just as smitten by her. I could see him grovelling.

"One more shot, pleaaasseee...?" he pleaded.

The girl nodded reluctantly and put down her bag. Then, in front of both of us, Fat Boy stood at the three-point line, and with a confident leap, he buried his ball in the net. It had taken him eighteen times to do it before The Vision showed up, and now suddenly, he had scored in one try.

Bloody show-off. His girlfriend clapped her hands with glee, and then pointed to her bag sitting on the floor. Fat Boy came over to pick it up, but he was such a klutz that he dropped it!

What tumbled out was a strange sight. I saw a glittery green-and-purple sequined fish tail on the ground. I looked at it with my jaw wide open a second time.

The girl giggled. She picked up the fish tail gently and shoved it into the bag. Then she looked at me and said in a conspiratorial whisper, "I turn into a mermaid when the moon is full."

Fat Boy and I couldn't help but guffaw. He then took the bag from her, picked up his basketball and walked off with her.

I looked as they retreated into the afternoon sun. A fat boy and his mermaid girlfriend. Well, what do you know.

ARIEL

Today, I met someone interesting! I noticed him as soon as I walked onto the basketball court. He had thick, brown hair cropped really tight. And oooh, what a lean body! There wasn't an ounce of fat on him. But it was his posture that drew my attention. He was leaning against the lamp post, watching Lasso like a hawk. He was tense, I could tell from his stiff shoulders.

When he played one-on-one with Lasso, I was really impressed. He was sleek, and he moved with an ease that I really liked. I was curious to see how he looked, so I yelled for Lasso.

When I went up closer to them, I saw that he was really, really cute. I was a little stunned, but I remembered to say "Hi". He stared at me, brooding and silent. He was too proud to say anything.

I was so conscious of myself that I pleaded with Lasso to go. But as always, he was clueless about the situation. He insisted, "One more shot, pleaaasseee...?" What could I say? So I waited while he took his time to get the ball into the net. By then, I was perspiring from anxiety. I was dying to leave immediately!

I could feel the boy staring hard at me. His gaze was so intent that I couldn't stop blushing. I signalled impatiently for Lasso to pick up my bag. He was sooooo clumsy that he had to drop it! I almost died when my mermaid costume fell out! I could see the boy was amused. He opened his mouth and grinned a little. I saw the smile and relaxed.

I giggled nervously and told him that I turn into a mermaid when the moon is full. He laughed! He actually did! AND HE LOOKED SOOOOO CUTE! The smile changed his face TOTALLY!

I stared at him till Lasso dragged me off. I hope I wasn't smiling like an idiot with my mouth wide open. I couldn't remember, really. As I walked off with Lasso, I couldn't help wondering if I would bump into him again.

4
Life in One of Singapore's Oldest Schools

Thomas S.R. Institute was set up a couple of years after the founding of Singapore in 1819. When I first got in, I realised that there are two distinct classes of students. One is an elite class whose parents are the top brass of society. These boys are also either really smart or naturally sporty. And they are worshipped by girls from convent schools.

There is another class of students, the majority of whom are ordinary boys from average, middle-class homes. Their only bragging right is that of being worshipped by their mothers for making it to the top boys' school in Singapore.

Unlike these boys, I belong to a third class. I am being brought up by a single mother, and I live in a rental flat. On top of that, I have a past hanging over me.

In the two weeks before I started school, I had been caught trading in stolen hand phones.

A policeman had caught me with the boys I played basketball with. Among the five of us, we had twelve hand phones stolen from unsuspecting people eating at various hawker centres. We were all sent to a police station, but I was the only one made to spend the night at the police station as my mother had refused to pick me up when I called. I was disappointed with her reaction, until I found out that she had spent the night trawling offices in Raffles Place, seeking advice from lawyers to save her son.

When I saw my mother in the juvenile court, I felt sorry. It wasn't because of how weary and disappointed she looked. It wasn't because her eyes were red and swollen from crying either. It was because I saw her bare wrist. My mother had taken off the only gift she had kept from my father – a gold bangle encrusted with precious stones.

From the time I was old enough to ask her about it, I had learnt that it was a family heirloom my father had given her in promise of a marriage that never materialised. She had worn it for as long as I could remember. I didn't know what she had done with it, but it must have been something to do with getting a lawyer to help me.

The lawyer argued passionately about my case in court. He managed to convince the judge that I deserved a second chance because I had been accepted into Thomas S.R. Institute. The poor judge looked ill at ease with my mother sobbing throughout the hearing. She even collapsed onto the floor at one point. The judge deliberated on my six years of primary school academic results, five trophies and a "Most Valuable Player" award. He finally dismissed me with a written warning on grounds of insufficient evidence.

But I wasn't stupid. I knew it was "Saint" Thomas, as the lawyer put it, and my mother's tears that had saved me. All my friends were sent to the Reformative Training Centre. But I was lucky, I got away. That night when we were home, I told my mother that I wouldn't give her any more trouble. My heart felt heavy as I saw her stroke her bare wrist. She said as tears welled up in her eyes, "I'm really proud you got into the school."

I know that surviving in school is going to be a real challenge. It isn't just the tough expectations placed on boys who are being groomed to excel – it is the ignominy of being born a bastard.

5
First Week of School

From the very first day, we were drilled on how clever and special we are. The school has an illustrious history of churning out leaders and captains of industry. We were told that we must uphold hereditary "rights" and display the same qualities that had made our predecessors proud.

But days after I started school, I got into trouble. I had overslept on a cold, rainy morning. My mother had already left for work and when I finally got out of bed, I realised to my horror that it was 7.15 am! School started at 7.35 am; there was no way I was going to make it in time. I would have stayed home, if not for the fact that I was anxious to go for the basketball team tryouts.

I rushed to get changed and carried my bicycle down four flights of stairs. The road was slippery and I had to cycle carefully.

By the time I got to school, it was almost 8.10 am. I knew the prefects would already be in class. So I took my time to lock up my bicycle before looking for a stretch of wall away from the main gates.

I leapt and grabbed the top edge of the wall. I swung my right leg over it, and just when my left leg crossed over, someone pulled me down from the other side. I collapsed on the ground and found myself sitting on wet mud.

I cursed and looked up. Staring into my face and smirking at my discomfort was none other than a prefect, his tie dangling in my face. He extended a hand to help me up.

"Name and class?" he asked.

I was furious at being caught. I slapped his hand away and straightened.

When I gave my name and class, he continued staring at me. Then he asked, "Have we met before?"

I looked at him blankly. I said, "This is my first time being caught late. I don't normally climb walls, so no, I haven't met you before."

The prefect's face changed. He said rudely, "I know you. We've fought before."

I looked hard at him. I really couldn't remember if we had fought in Fight Club before. He looked too decent to be one of the street kids who played basketball with me, so it couldn't be that either. But he did look vaguely familiar. Fair with a high forehead and sharp cheekbones. Lean and athletic-looking. Probably attractive to girls, but his arrogance was overbearing.

"Sorry, I've got class. I'd love to hang around to chat, but I can't," I said.

The prefect took his time to write down my name and class. Then he looked up.

"I know your name's not Aron. Don't lie to me!" he threatened.

I wished I didn't blush, but I could feel the heat creeping up my neck. Giving a false name to get out of trouble was a trick I had always used.

"Ayush Lee," I said after a long beat. The smirk returned to his face.

"What are you, Chinese or Indian?" he asked in a derogatory manner. Then he slammed his notebook shut, thought for a bit, and spat out, "I remember you! We fought in the playground when we were kids!"

Suddenly it all came back. That time I was nine. The boy who had pushed my face into the sand. His mother who had humiliated mine at my flat. Yes, it was Edward.

"What a small world," I said sarcastically. I bolted in the direction of my classroom. I didn't turn back to look at Edward. It was only the first week of school and I had already made an enemy.

That afternoon, I met Edward again at the basketball court. I found out he was a year older and in Secondary Two. He wasn't just a prefect; he was also captain of the lower secondary basketball team.

There were only two spots open to Secondary One students. We were told to play basketball in three rounds of games. The coach picked out boys who would advance into the second and third rounds.

I was beat by the time I got into the last round. It was down to five Secondary One students in the final round. And guess who was among them? Fat Boy! I half expected his mermaid girlfriend to appear and cheer us on. Fat Boy didn't acknowledge me. But he was friendly enough to watch my back as we played against our seniors. We made a good team.

In the last quarter of the game, Coach blew the whistle. I saw Edward making a swop with a boy going out. I had an uneasy feeling as he gave me a mean look.

The ball was in play. Edward received the ball. He drove it towards our net, with me and Fat Boy pounding after him. Cutting him off, I stopped him at the three-point line. Seeing that he was about to make a shot, I waited in anticipation, arms raised high. Edward jumped; I forced myself to rise higher. With almost superhuman strength, I lifted my arm just barely an inch higher and blocked his shot. I saw Edward's shocked face.

I then charged towards his net. It was a turnover and fast break. Fat Boy came running to support me. As I got into the box, I saw Edward coming to cut me off. I tossed the ball at Fat Boy and he caught it deftly. With a casual jump, he buried it.

I grinned and yelled, "Yo! Fat Boy, my hero!"

We didn't score any more balls after that, but I gained a few rough knocks from Edward. At one point, I was so angry that I jabbed my elbow hard into his ribs. Coach blew a warning whistle. I thought he was going to yell "Foul!" but he didn't. Instead, he stopped the match. I was actually relieved as I was going to collapse.

Coach told Fat Boy and me that we had made the cut. But he had a few words for me.

"I know you're good. But I won't tolerate rough play in my court," he said.

I bristled at his unjust remarks. It was Edward who kept bumping into me! But I knew when to keep my mouth shut. So I just nodded.

When I saw Fat Boy in the toilet, he was lounging on a bench eating a Mars bar. I was happy to see a friendly face. I extended a hand in front of him and said, "Excellent play!" Imagine my surprise when he simply stood up and walked away from my outstretched hand.

Just before he stepped out of the toilet, he said over his shoulder, "The name's Lasso. Don't *ever* call me fat."

Well, what do you know. Fat Boy had spunk. I smiled to myself.

Lasso

In my family, boys are regarded as superheroes. It's not like we have to wear tights or do incredible feats; our mothers just like to think that we are special. My grandfather, my father and all my uncles were obsessed with playing basketball in the Philippines. Everyone back home expects me to join a basketball league one day, something that will take me to playing pro for the sport.

But I have a problem. I weigh 176 pounds – that's 80 kg or 16 sacks of unwashed rice bound together. Which doesn't just make me overweight, I am classified as SERIOUSLY OBESE in a medical examination. Technically when I play basketball, I can keel over any time from heart fatigue. Now if you think that's lame, wait till you hear this.

I get the sort of physical discomfort that plagues boys, five to six times a day! And it's a real problem, because good Catholic boys are not supposed to think about the s__ word, but I can't help it, it's puberty!

I know what nasty boys call me behind my back; I just ignore them. Lately, I've been finding comfort in reading. It helps to make sense of the bewilderment I feel. I hate my studies and I can't wait to get away from my mother's incessant nagging. The only thing that keeps me going is basketball! I'm so pleased that I got into the school team. Now I just have to play hard and get selected for the Thomas Titans League! Nothing can possibly stop me from achieving my goal. Not even this new boy, Ayush. I heard the boys say that he was captain of his primary school team. Well, even if he's really that good, he'll only be second best to me.

6
Back to the Mermaid

Lasso and I were in different classes, but we shared one common classroom for Literature. My class was reading *Julius Caesar*. *But, for my own part, it was Greek to me.*

I knew Lasso had sat in the desk before me. How did I guess? There were at least five carvings of the name "Ariel" all over the desk top! They were so tiny that you would have missed them if you weren't looking. I was amused to see one that read, "Lasso ♥ Ariel". Man, he was really infatuated with the mermaid!

That day after school, I caught up with Lasso outside the school gates. He was waiting for his ride. I decided to say "Hi".

"Was that your girlfriend at the basketball court?" I asked.

Lasso looked at me suspiciously. "Why are you asking?"

I grinned and said, "She's cool. What did you have to do, catch her from the sea with a lasso?"

Lasso burst out laughing. That broke the ice and I laughed along with him. When he stopped, he just shrugged and said, "She has a role in a play. She's playing..."

"...the little mermaid!" we said in unison. We laughed again.

Lasso added, "I met her when I first came to Singapore. In church."

I nodded encouragingly. He continued, "I accompany her to rehearsals as she's quite nervous during acting."

"Are there lots of speaking lines?" I asked. I had never watched a play before and I was curious.

Lasso blurted out, "Come and watch! I'm seeing her tomorrow. She could do with more moral support!"

I nodded happily. That sounded really cool. Then a car arrived for Lasso. It was an old beat-up BMW 7 series – an ancient blue model with grey tinted windows. Well, it was still a car. Lasso got chauffeured while I had to take the bus or cycle.

"My dad's here. See you tomorrow!" Lasso said, scooting off with an apologetic wave.

I looked as he got into the car. His father looked like a bigger version of him. A Eurasian-looking guy with thick wiry hair and a friendly chubby face. Lasso's father nodded and smiled at me. I said "Hi". As the car pulled away from me, I was overwhelmed with jealousy. I had no father to pick me up.

—

I am stranded on an island. There is a full moon and I can see the cold mist rising from the surface of the dark, choppy waters. I hear a sweet melodious voice echoing from a distance. I turn in the direction of the voice. There, again. The strains of a song...

"In the night when I swim
Not far from the land
I spy a lad, a lovely boy with dark hair
With a comb in my hand..."

Something jumps out of the water. It's swimming towards me. I can't see what it is. It's too dark. Faster now, the shape moves, keeping just below the surface. I walk out into the shallow waters. The waves hit against my thighs as I dig my feet deeper into the sand. Suddenly, the movement stops just a metre away from me.

As I hold my breath waiting for it to emerge, the moon casts a silvery light on a vision rising from the waters. It is Ariel, beautiful with a luminous glow, and totally naked! She smiles at me alluringly as she raises her arms and squeezes water from her hair. Then she reveals a comb in her hand and runs it through her hair.

I turn away from her, embarrassed at her lack of modesty. I feel something hit against my body. I look down into the water and I see a green-and-purple sequined fish tail. It coils around my body. It goes tighter and tighter until I want to scream! Ariel's face turns into a nasty leer. It morphs into an ugly contorted scowl till...it looks like Edward!

"Argghhhh!" I screamed in fear as I sat up in bed. I looked around me. It was dark and I was totally drenched in sweat. I heard a hurried rustling of bedspread. Mum bumped her head against the ceiling of my upper bunk bed. She cursed loudly as she scrambled out of her bed. She put her arm reassuringly over my back. I felt calmer after a while.

"Sorry, Mum. Just a silly nightmare," I said. Mum nodded in understanding.

"Are you worried about school?" she asked with concern.

I shrugged and said, "Nothing I can't handle."

She stayed for a few more minutes, and then went back to bed. I managed a smile to assure her. Stupid Edward. Why did he have to spoil a perfectly erotic wet dream?

—

She has a hauntingly beautiful voice, singing a hymn as old as the call of sirens that causes sailors to run their ship aground.

When I saw Ariel the next day at the rehearsal, I couldn't stop thinking about my wet dream.

The year was the twentieth anniversary of Walt Disney's *The Little Mermaid* animated feature release. The drama school which Ariel attended was putting up a play to ride on the event.

Just looking at Ariel made me all hot and bothered. I could see that Lasso worshipped the ground she walked on. All she had to do was look his way and he would fetch her a glass of water or a pen for her to take notes when the director gave comments on her acting. I sat in one of the front rows studying the intricate set of a nineteenth-century ship.

Ariel didn't have her mermaid tail on, but the image from the night before stuck in my brain like a stamp. She had on a white translucent shirt, and I could vaguely make out her shapely silhouette each time she moved into the spotlight. I enjoyed her acting. She was so earnest, and her voice rang clear and sweet when she read her lines. I was so captivated that I jumped when Lasso patted me on the shoulder. I looked at him sheepishly, glad that it was too dark for him to see I was blushing.

"Know who's playing the prince?" he asked suddenly.

"You?" I suggested mischievously. He shook his head resignedly.

"It's that senior boy who played against us in the basketball selection."

I looked at him blankly. *This can't be happening. Not just in my dream, but in real life too?*

Edward came on stage at the end of Act I. He played an overly dramatic, highly-strung prince living out his last moments in a shipwreck. He shrieked like a banshee as he stood on the deck of the ship. It was only a rehearsal, for goodness' sake!

My eardrums were still ringing after he leapt off from a pitiful height of one metre from the deck. He then rolled clumsily into the waiting hands of Ariel. She enveloped him in an embrace, and cradled his head in her bosom.

I felt Lasso stiffening beside me. A curse escaped from his mouth. I grinned. I was glad there was someone else who felt like murdering Edward. I had found my partner in crime.

—

Ariel

I was sooooo excited today! I saw the boy from the basketball court! And guess what? Lasso said they are in the same school! I can't believe how lucky I am. Hmmm... I wonder if he has a girlfriend. He looks like someone girls will happily throw themselves at.

I tried to spy on him discreetly. But it was really tough as the spotlight was always shining into my eyes. Each time I turned to look in his direction, I could see him studying the ship behind us. Oh please! Surely our readings were much more interesting than an ancient nineteenth-century ship! I couldn't tell if he had enjoyed my performance. Lasso said it was his first time at a rehearsal. I wished we had time to chat; I would have loved to ask what he thought of my acting.

But I do know his name now. It's Ayush Lee. And something tells me I'll be seeing a lot more of him from now.

7
Blast From the Past

We got an unusual peek at life in the nineteenth century today. A few classes of Secondary One students were assembled to witness the "unearthing" of a treasure trove found on the ground floor of the teachers' common room. It was quite a laugh, as it was only an old tin trunk measuring half a metre all round. The trunk had been discovered in an unused storeroom. The teachers suspected it had been kept there since the late 1890s.

It had taken four men to remove a reclining wall hiding a secret compartment in the storeroom. The mound of stone debris stood at four-feet high after the wall was knocked down and broken into slabs. The musty smell of dank stonewalls permeated the air as, class after class, we gathered around the space to peek at the trunk.

One boy screamed when a tiny snake crawled out of the mound. That seemed to break the tension in the air. Boisterous boys then started laughing and shoving one another. A couple of superstitious students muttered something about offering incense, suggesting that there could be skeletal remains of the trunk's custodian lying nearby. The workmen didn't find any.

I overheard the teachers exclaiming how ironic it was that we owed the find to a modern-day problem. The land behind the schoolyard had been reclaimed by the land transport authority. Because of its decision to widen the road, the entire building housing the teachers' common room had to go. And so the trunk had surfaced.

I rifled through the contents of the trunk. It was obviously an Englishman who had compiled the secret stash. Evidence of our British colonial past was so obvious! There was a poster of The Royal Aquarium Theatre, located in Westminster, London. Dated 1898, the Theatre offered, for a shilling, a performance by "a Minstrel Dog Orchestra, dogs playing drums, cymbals and various instruments, and Talking Donkeys doing all sorts of marvellous things blindfolded"!

Another find was a copy of *The Telegraph*, dated April 9, 1899. Titled "The Essential Paris à la mode", the article discussed the well-cut Paris skirt. Described as "neither skimpy nor raggy, it is accurately shaped to the hip, but so cut on the bias that it looks neither tight nor strained. This same bias causes it to fall in graceful flutes from the knees, resting well on the ground, and measuring about four yards round the hem". I laughed when I read a line that said the length of the skirt was "to prevent tripping and stumbling, which was neither dignified nor elegant".

But what really arrested my attention was news from the sports pages. There were pages and pages on cricket, and one particular article dated 1895 caught my eye. An Englishman by the name of W.G. Grace was changing the standard of batsmanship. Before his time, it was unusual to score fifty on the rough wickets of the day and most rare to gain a century. But Grace was making centuries and double centuries.

At the beginning of the 1895 season, Grace was forty-six years old. He made his hundredth century in first-class cricket, batting for Gloucestershire against Somerset. By May 30, he had reached his thousandth run of the season, and was greeted enthusiastically in the field and in the press. Even The Prince of Wales wrote to congratulate him. Awesome!

I wished I had more time to browse through the trunk's contents, but the teachers hurried us and my class had to leave. For no reason, I started thinking about courting rituals back in the nineteenth century. If people had no movies to watch back then, what did men and women do on dates? Ride around the Singapore Botanic Gardens in horse-drawn carriages, boring each other to tears?

When it was recess time, I sneaked off to find Lasso. I saw him in a corner of the schoolyard by himself, reading a book. He almost fell off from the edge of the wooden table when I snatched the book out of his hands. I read the title, *How To Read A Girl's Mind*. I cocked an eyebrow and tried hard not to laugh. When Lasso grabbed the book back angrily, I let it go.

"You're sooo rude! Get lost!" he yelled. His face was flushed and he looked hurt. I felt sorry. But I didn't let it show. I shrugged nonchalantly and walked off.

—

I volunteered to clean the trunk at the end of the day. The teacher gave precise instructions on how every article should be recorded and photographed.

From the Trunk of Relics, these were the items that were hoarded by an old Englishman.

- Posters advertising performances at The Royal Aquarium Theatre. Listed performers included the Polar Walrus, Mademoiselle Paula and the Tank of Huge Alligators and Snakes, the Russian Giantess, the Wonderful One-Legged Acrobat, Captain Costentenus Tattooed from Head to Foot in Chinese Tartary, and the Cannibals of Tierra del Fuego ("fed at 2.30, 6.00 and 10.00"). Awesome! Did they like to feed on human remains?

- Books. One which caught my eye was a copy of a play written by Henrik Ibsen, titled *Ghosts*, dated 1891. Ha! Who would have thought they were into "ghosts" back then?
- Cricket news in *The Daily Telegraph*
- A photo of the European members of the Singapore Cricket Club, taken after a lawn tennis competition, dated 1894
- Ink pot and writing instruments
- Envelopes with affixed stamps (with letters still in them!)

I studied the stamps. I looked around me. I couldn't believe that they hadn't planted a guard to watch over the contents of the trunk. It was just me and the ancient "treasures"? I was incredulous. These things should be worth a tonne of money!

I looked at the items more carefully. The stamps were postmarked around 1899; they were half-penny stamps printed with the bust head of Queen Victoria. The ink pot was useless, and so were the writing instruments. The photo could fetch some money, but it would be too obvious to steal it. I sifted through the stack of books. Boring titles. And none in mint condition. I doubted they would fetch much. Finally I let out a huge sigh. I guessed the teachers had calculated the exact material worth of the contents of the trunk. It was practically zero.

After I was done with my task, I packed everything in two cardboard cartons. As I closed the lid on one of the boxes, something caught my eye. A book with the title *Mr Humphry's Book of Love Secrets*.

Lasso's hurt look crossed my mind. I looked at the book and flipped through it quickly. Guess no one would miss it.

I also took one letter from the stack of envelopes. For my bedtime reading amusement.

I tucked the book and letter under the waistband of my trousers. I lifted the two boxes and took them to the staff room. I left the boxes where I was told to return them.

8

A Sunday Letter & *Mr Humphry's Book of Love Secrets*

The Englishman must have sent his son to a boarding school back in England. The letter I brought home was one of many Sunday letters the boy wrote. He described vivid scenes of bullies and cheats, cowards and sneaks. I read about the boy's hard and lumpy bed which sagged in the middle, the peeling linoleum on his dormitory floor, the cold showers after cricket practice and the indignity of having to clean the cricket boots of his seniors.

He even described one incident when he had to sit on a cracked toilet seat that pinched his bottom. It was a refreshing blast from the past to hear a school boy's ranting, so similar to the pains I was experiencing in school. But I was jealous of the boy's description of summer, when he talked about long, lazy afternoons playing village cricket with his father.

After I was through with the letter, I read the book I had stolen: *Mr Humphry's Book of Love Secrets*, published in 1891.

The Etiquette of Courting

Carpe Diem. There is nothing more to be said than to seize the day, gather ye rosebuds, eat, drink and be merry. In the case of winning a lady's hand, pursue these three principles of life: consideration, respect and sincerity.

What an ancient book! It was almost midnight when I started reading. My favourite chapter was the "*Five Deadly Sins of Boyish Behaviour*".

Spitting

Most men excel in this art. There is something primal about coughing up phlegm and aiming to hit a target. But while men enjoy exerting their male dominance through spitting, women hate it.

If you see a lovable hare while racked with a spasm of phlegm, can you bring yourself to spit at it? So when you are walking arm-in-arm with a woman, think of the white hare and do not let the spit fly.

Even if you are alone, refrain from spitting as you never know which woman is watching you secretly.

Passing Gas

A rite of passage for growing boys, passing gas like a trumpet is a great esteem booster. But while this skill may help you score with male thirteen-year-olds, it will not impress the girl around you.

So what do you do when you are with a girl and the urge rides up? Hold it in! Or ask to be excused. Retire to the bathroom and pass it out. Never pass gas in front of a girl. She will not be able to forgive you.

Scratching

Every man will understand why there is a need to scratch or adjust his "privates" once in a while.

The question you should ask yourself is, how do you do this discreetly without annoying the woman? The trick is to turn away from her, or do it under the table. If you understand that she does not wish to see you scratch, then you will not do it in front of her. If you really have to "grab and move", do it in the bathroom.

Nose Picking

You cannot stop a sneeze, but you can avoid picking your nose in front of the lady.

Just like how burping and passing of gas are a matter of self-control, refrain from sticking your finger in your nose. Such behaviour is best left to the confines of the bathroom.

Bad Breath

This can arise either from poor teeth-brushing or vile gases in the stomach. Bad breath is the most powerful dent in a woman's first impression. Brush your teeth before meeting a woman. If you really need to know if your breath smells, ask your mother.

I was so engrossed in reading, I didn't get to bed till 4 am! Nothing in the world could have persuaded me to sell this book. The manual was written for the likes of Lasso! When he's through with this, he's going to make Edward look like a clod beside him. We'll see who Ariel is going to like, a polished gem or a snooty piece of shit.

9
Making Up

I saw Lasso the next day after school. He was standing outside a lingerie shop in a shopping mall. It was obvious he wanted to step into the shop, but didn't dare to. When he saw me, he turned red. I took one look at the bras and panties hanging prettily in neat rows, and shook my head. I placed my hand in my bag and pulled out *Mr Humphry's Book of Love Secrets*. I shoved it in his face.

"Read it. Read everything!" I said tersely. I turned to walk away. But Lasso grabbed my arm.

"You've got to help me, please," he pleaded desperately.

"What? Choose a bra?" I mocked him. I was exasperated at how wheedling he was. This wasn't the Lasso I knew at the basketball court.

"Look, I can guess you're crazy over Ariel. But it's not cool to be looking at girlie things! If anyone from school catches you here, you're dead," I warned.

Lasso bent his head, thinking. He twirled a wiry strand of hair furiously with a finger. Then he looked up and grinned.

"I can always say I'm getting a present for my mother," he said hopefully.

I rolled my eyes. I couldn't believe I was even having a conversation with him. In front of a bra shop. I looked at him for a long beat.

"Why are you really here?" I asked finally.

"Ariel needs a push-up bra! I have to get it for her! If she doesn't... you know, make her bust bigger, she gets cut from the play!"

I stared incredulously at him. I weighed what he said. Was he kidding me?

"Why can't she get it for herself?" I asked.

"It's expensive. She doesn't have the money for it," Lasso said with his voice down to a whisper.

I stared at him again. I couldn't believe Ariel was talking to Lasso about how expensive it was to buy a bra. I poked hard at his chest.

"Don't lie to me. She wouldn't be telling you all this!" I retorted.

Lasso massaged his chest tenderly and shrugged unhappily.

"Edward was bragging about cutting Ariel out of the play. He said she wasn't busty enough to play a mermaid," he spat out. "She's hurt. I just want to help her look good."

The dream of Ariel came back to haunt me. I recalled how alluring she had looked in her nakedness. I shook the image out of my head. I turned to look around the mall. I wanted to make sure there wasn't anyone we knew from school. I signalled to him to remove his school badge. He unpinned it eagerly. I pocketed my own badge and untucked my shirt from my trousers. Lasso was clutching *Mr Humphry's Book of Love Secrets* to his chest, looking at me like a lost puppy.

I sauntered into the lingerie shop. Lasso followed right behind me. I smiled at the first sales assistant the moment she came up to me. I could see she was trying hard not to smirk.

"Can I help you?" she asked.

I nodded at Lasso.

"My friend needs to buy his girlfriend a present. Can you recommend something?" I asked, trying to sound as adult-like as possible.

She looked at him suspiciously. "Do you have money?" she asked.

Lasso nodded quickly. He whipped out a debit card from his pocket and flashed it in her face. I felt a stab of jealousy. My mother had never applied for a credit card in her life. She probably didn't qualify for one, earning little in her job as a secretary.

The salesgirl looked doubtfully at Lasso.

"Do you know her size?" she asked gently.

Lasso looked perplexed. He shook his head. Then his eyes settled on me and before I knew it, I felt myself blushing as his words tumbled out. "She's about his size! He could wear a bra her size!"

I felt my ears burn. I glared at Lasso furiously. By now, two other assistants in the shop had joined the first salesgirl. They were obviously thrilled to be part of my embarrassment. There was no way I was going to let them put a bra on me! I turned angrily to Lasso.

"I'm leaving!" I hissed. I was mad for having my goodwill betrayed. I remembered to snatch *Mr Humphry's Book of Love Secrets* from him before I walked out of the store.

I left Lasso to gesticulate to the salesgirls how large Ariel's bosom was. As I turned a corner, I saw Edward and his cronies heading towards me. The same four boys who were always trailing behind him. Faceless creatures.

I didn't even know their names. Edward saw me and cocked an eyebrow.

"Alone?" he asked mockingly.

I barely glanced at him when I shot out sarcastically, "No, I left my boyfriend in the lingerie shop."

I continued walking for a couple of minutes before I realised the horror of my statement. I turned and ran back to the shop. Five metres from the lingerie shop, I saw Lasso standing in front of a long mirror, wearing a bra over his school shirt. *Oh man!* And he was admiring himself in the mirror!

Edward and his four cronies were standing just outside the shop, hands poised in the air, recording the scene with their hand phones. Edward was the first to spot me. He gave me a thumbs-up sign as he mouthed just one word, "Faggot."

I seethed as the five of them brushed past me, smirking and laughing as they walked off.

I looked as Lasso preened himself. He was unaware of what had just happened. He pushed the green-and-purple sequined bra higher up his chest. The three salesgirls were fawning all over him. Finally I heard him yell, "She's going to love it!"

Lasso

Life in the Philippines was tough. I spent the first six years of my life in a poor province. The men in my family fished for a living, but seriously at heart, all they really wanted to do was to play basketball. I missed the simple life in the village. We used to play basketball on dirt courts, ride four to a motorcycle and chase wild cackling hens and stray dogs through the village.

All children shared something common in childhood; it was the trauma of having tapeworms breed in our bodies. Pooping tapeworms in a hole in the ground used to be my forte; I was called the "King of Poopworm" for being able to churn out the biggest mound of tapeworm-entangled shit in the entire village!

But if there was anything more exciting than that, it must be the vivid memory of seeing women wash their clothes in the river. My mother used to leave me to catch tadpoles in the shallow waters by the river bank. After the women were done scrubbing out the grime and rinsing their clothes in the water, they would strip and have a bath. I used to gawk unabashedly at their womanly assets! My mother eventually stopped bringing me on her river trips.

Then my father got drafted into the prestigious ASEAN Basketball League to play pro; that brought the entire family out to Malaysia. When I got accepted into Thomas S.R. Institute on an ASEAN Schools' Scholarship, we moved to Singapore.

The moment I stumbled on the green-and-purple sequined bra in the shop, I knew I had to buy it. It brought back memories of my childhood. The colour of the fabric reminded me of the shallow waters of the river bank where I used to catch tadpoles.

10
In Love

Sick and pining for love, the little mermaid approaches the old sea witch for a magic potion to turn her fish tail into legs. She wants to go ashore to see the prince she saved. But it comes with a heavy price; she has to trade her lovely voice for the potion.

I followed Lasso to Ariel's second rehearsal in a week. I was feeling guilty for having set Edward on his trail. I didn't mention that Edward and his cronies had taken pictures, or probably even filmed him wearing the bra. What he didn't know wouldn't hurt.

The old hag playing the sea witch was really a boy dressed in a Halloween costume. Lasso was so full of these backstage trivia. I could see he was excited to pass Ariel her gift. When she came around to see him during a break, he almost tripped in his anxiety to meet her.

She smiled at him fondly as she opened the box. When she saw the green-and-purple sequined bra, her face lit up. She squealed like a small girl, holding the bra to her chest.

I turned away, feeling embarrassed when the image of my dream came back.

Then out of the corner of my eye, I saw Edward making his way over. The hair on the back of my neck stood as he drawled in a mocking tone, "Pretty. It matches your tail perfectly!"

I narrowed my eyes at Edward, shaking my head as a warning. He looked at me slyly before facing Ariel. "You'll need all the help you can get to make you look all woman!" he said, mimicking the shape of a large bosom.

I saw Ariel's face crumpling. She turned to Lasso and cried, "He's so mean!"

I could see Lasso seething with rage. He patted Ariel's back comfortingly, looking at me for support. But words failed me. The guilt of what I had done to Lasso weighed heavily. We watched as Edward walked away, head held high. How I wished I could kick his butt.

When I came out after the rehearsal, I saw Edward waiting for me outside the building. He was leaning against a wall, scuffing his sneaker in the dirt.

He straightened when he saw me. He had an evil look on his face when he opened his mouth.

"Does he know we have pictures?" he asked.

I shook my head. I was pissed at being trapped.

"It's going to cost you if you want the pictures back," he offered. I thought hard. How did I get involved in this? I shook my head nonchalantly.

"I don't give a damn. You can do anything you want with the pictures," I retorted and turned my back.

Edward shrieked with laughter as I walked away. "You're such a loyal buddy!"

Ariel

> It was such a horrid day! I was terribly and horribly humiliated beyond words! That Edward! How could he embarrass me in front of Ayush! And to think that Lasso had spent a bomb getting me a bustier to match my mermaid costume!
>
> I can't believe I used to have a crush on Edward! Like most of the girls in our acting class, I found him handsome. I felt really special when he picked me to play the

mermaid. Edward has always been appointed the lead actor in our plays. And because his father contributes most of the money to put up our performances, the drama teacher panders to him. Like a besotted puppy!

Edward and I went out a few times, mostly for an ice cream or a burger after acting class. But I never did like seeing him look at other girls while he was with me. I found it really annoying.

And he had this irritating habit of forgetting to call when he said he would. I hated the feeling of anxiety each time I sat by the phone, waiting for him to call. And when he did, he would always have a lousy excuse. Like the time he said he would call me by 10 pm but never did. I actually waited till 2 am before giving up!

When I saw him in acting class the next day, he said he was playing computer games and had forgotten. That was when I decided to stop going out with him. Not like he cared;

he was soon hitting on other girls in the class. I was hurt but I got over him fast.

Lasso, on the other hand, is different! I like going out with him. He's always doing things for me. All I have to do is look in his direction, and he will know what I need. He seems to be able to read my mind instantly! I call him my big cuddly bear; he's someone I would trust totally.

AYUSH. I was excited to see him, of course! I got carried away when I saw Lasso's gift. The bustier was sooooo pretty! When I held it against my chest, I was surprised to see Ayush turn away. I was pleased to see that. I never thought he would be so decent! Almost like a gentleman. He must have been very well brought up by his mother. I can imagine him to be really caring when he's out with a girl. I tried asking Lasso several times if he has a girlfriend. But he wouldn't tell me. He seemed unhappy every time I mentioned Ayush's name.

11
Training

Lasso had a surprise for me when we showed up for basketball training. He flashed a gleaming set of braces in a good-natured smile at me. I chuckled and clubbed him on the shoulder.

"How do you eat? Can you even chew?" I cried out.

He suddenly looked all serious. "The bigger question is, can I kiss a girl?"

We both laughed and then fell into step around the court to warm up.

When Coach appeared, he screamed, "Are you wimps? Faster!"

The first drill was a marathon. Something must have pissed him off that morning. He made us do one hundred laps around the court. We were twelve boys in singlets and black shorts panting under the hot sun, running at five metres per second. After fifty-one laps, two boys dropped out. Six other boys dropped out shortly after that. It was down to just Lasso, me, Edward and one of his cronies.

When we got to the ninety-eighth lap, I pumped up the speed till I was leading the pack. From the corner of my eye, I saw Edward following hot on my heels. He overtook me and finished the last lap ahead of all of us.

I grinned wickedly when I folded over to catch my breath. I knew what was coming. And I was right. Coach made the four of us play full-court two-on-two. He was in a really bad mood. Must have quarrelled with his girlfriend. Definitely that or he had had a rough day with the principal, his boss.

Coach threw me the ball and yelled, "Go!"

I grabbed the ball and dribbled down the court. Edward stole the ball right out of my hands. I pounded after him but I was too slow. He dunked it before I was even close. I couldn't believe it! What was he, some kind of machine? He wasn't even tired! Even the last sprint I had forced him into didn't affect him.

"Go again!" Coach screamed.

This time, Edward's crony had the ball. I played defence. I crouched down low, and spread my arms and legs wide and high. But I didn't see it coming. The monster just bowled me over. He was that huge. I heard the whistle and found myself on my back. I looked up and saw Lasso bending over me. All I could think of was how shiny his braces looked.

I took his hand and straightened. Coach barely glanced at me.

"Go!" he shouted. What's eating him, I thought furiously.

This time, Edward charged towards me when Coach threw me the ball. He screamed like a banshee, trying to intimidate me. I dribbled with my right hand. When he reached for the ball, I spun-dribbled around him, did a three-sixty, and raced down the court. He was right behind me. I saw Lasso ahead. He signalled for me to pass him the ball. I ignored him. Then I stopped fifteen feet from the hoop. I made a pretty little jump shot and buried the ball. Edward was furious!

He did a quick start passing the ball, and his crony charged towards our basket. Lasso moved forward to cut him off.

Then I saw it happening in slow motion. A few feet from the basket, Lasso managed to knock the ball out of his hand. As Edward's crony turned to attack, he smashed his elbow into Lasso's cheek. Lasso fell and landed on his arm awkwardly. I heard the crack of bone from where I stood. His inhuman shriek froze me.

When I recovered, I ran towards him. Coach got to him first. As Lasso lay in an undignified heap, he opened his mouth to whimper. I saw a bloodied mess of braces mixed with flesh. It wasn't pretty. I felt sick.

When Coach ran to get help, Lasso passed out. I looked around and barked at the closest boy to remove his singlet. I rolled it into a heap and slipped it under Lasso's head gently. It was the least I could do to protect him from the scorching ground. Edward was standing just beside me. I heard him mutter two words, "Bloody faggot."

Very calmly I turned around to face him. I sucker punched him and had the pleasure of hearing him cry in pain. His cronies came immediately to his rescue. They held me back as I tried to lay a kick in his groin. My street fighting instinct surfaced as I twisted and freed myself from their clasp. I chased him down the court and pounced on him.

As he fell to the ground looking at me fearfully, I raised my fist and brought it down to his face. But I stopped just before I connected. It was the look of absolute terror on his face. It reminded me of my mother's face. She had that same look of a frightened rabbit when she faced the judge in the juvenile court.

Because of my momentary hesitation, Edward seized the chance. He punched me in the chin. That snapped me out of my daze. But before I could retaliate, four pairs of strong arms were pulling me back. It was his cronies again.

By then, Coach had returned with medical help. Their attention was focused on getting Lasso to the sick bay. I was alone with Edward and his friends.

Edward held his nose gingerly. He straightened and cast a menacing look at me. He spat at my feet as his cronies held me tight.

"You bloody Chindian! You're going to pay for this!" He gestured to his bloodied nose.

I just smiled coldly at him.

12
The Little Mermaid and Her Prince

She is dumb; she can neither sing nor speak, but she captures the prince's heart with her graceful ways. She dances oh so beautifully; but what the prince doesn't know is that with every step she takes, she seems to be treading on sharp knives. This is the curse she has to endure in exchange for the prince's love. In the night when the prince is asleep, the little mermaid soaks her feet in water, crying as she washes her bloodstained feet.

Lasso was lying in hospital with a broken arm. He had texted me to go watch Ariel at her rehearsal. I sat in the dark watching her comb out her hair and wash her feet. She had an ethereal quality about her as she acted. I felt guilty that Lasso wasn't with me. It felt like I was intruding on a private moment.

When she came to find me after her rehearsal, she looked shocked to see my bruise.

"That must be really painful," she pointed at my chin. I shrugged and grinned. I thought quickly. Surely she wouldn't want to hear that I had got beaten up.

"I fell," I lied. She left it at that.

"You were very good," I said shyly. She smiled at me happily.

"What happened to Lasso?" she asked.

"Broke his arm during basketball practice," I replied. She gasped.

"He's fine," I said, then added reassuringly, "The nurses think he's cute."

Ariel smiled and asked if I could wait for her while she changed.

She was wearing a figure-hugging T and a pair of skinny jeans when she came out of the building. I took one look at her chest and blushed furiously. I offered to walk her to the bus stop.

As I walked beside her, I cursed my raging hormones. I started thinking of what she was wearing under the shirt. When she turned to look at me knowingly, my heart lurched. My brain raced, and finally I thought of a paragraph I had read in *Mr Humphry's Book of Love Secrets*. I had left the book with Lasso in hospital. But I remembered it line for line.

To cultivate the art of conversation, you need like minds and kindred spirits. Think of something sincere to say. Forget perfect one-liners, there are none. Say something true. If the girl senses that you are honest, she will warm up to you. Talk to her as you would to your best friend. It is not difficult to assume that she has read a book or done something you have enjoyed too.

"So, watched any movies lately?" I blurted out.

She raised an eyebrow. "Are you trying to ask me out?" she said and grinned.

I blushed again. "I'm only saying what Lasso would have asked you."

She thought for a while before she shook her head. "Nope. Too busy with rehearsals."

When we reached the bus stop, she tugged at my sleeve and pulled me down to sit beside her. We started chatting about all the things we liked. I realised we had a lot in common. We loved movies like *Ice Age, Charlie and the Chocolate Factory* and *Pirates of the Caribbean.* And I was surprised to learn that she enjoyed books which we were forced to read for Literature, like *Lord of the Flies*! So I was not the only oddball around.

As for music, Ariel's crazy about boy bands like Take That, Boyzone and Westlife. Like me, she thought it was the best thing on earth that the older bands were making a comeback after so many years. I told her my mum used to be a fan of Take That, when they were a teenage boy band. She laughed with rounded eyes and cried out, "She must be really young!"

I nodded proudly. "People mistake her for my older sister."

"What's the one song you really like?" she asked, all serious suddenly.

I thought hard. "'*No Matter What*'. Boyzone."

She grinned and whispered, "Me too."

I looked at her happily. We liked the same song.

I looked at my watch after what seemed like a long time. Ariel laughed out loud when she saw my surprised face. We had talked for more than two hours!

"You didn't even realise I'd missed seven buses!" she cried out. I looked even more shocked. Then I started laughing along with her. I sat there staring at her face. I felt my heart squeezing. She was so pretty and sincere. Then my thoughts turned to Lasso lying in hospital. His mouth had swelled to twice its normal size. The braces had cut into his flesh during the accident. His arm was broken and placed in a cast.

This is wrong, I panicked. Lasso should be here with her, not me. I froze when Ariel touched me lightly on the face.

"First, purple. Next, green and yellow!" she giggled. Her touch felt so soft and gentle.

"It's not that bad," I managed to croak.

"Did you see a doctor?" she asked with concern.

"Nope," I whispered. I felt really uncomfortable. Somewhere, I had crossed an imaginary line. This is the girl whom Lasso adores, I kept telling myself. This is wrong, wrong, wrong!

Before I could stop myself, I grabbed her wrist. I held her firmly and stared into her eyes. She blushed a pretty pink. But she didn't remove her wrist from my clasp. It was the bus that broke the magic. Sputtering in fits and starts, it stopped just in front of us.

Ariel whispered, "No 8. My lucky number."

I nodded dumbly. "Better go," I said.

My eyes burned after her as she got on the bus. As it pulled away, I felt an incredible urge to get up and run. Suddenly I shot up from my seat. I ran after the bus. I shouted to Ariel and she heard me. She stood up and poked her face out of the window. She laughed, waving at me madly. I ran after the bus for about two hundred metres.

All the time, Ariel was egging me on, her head hanging out of the bus, her hair flying in the wind. She was oblivious to the unamused stares of strangers. I was touched by her nonchalance and that only spurred me to keep running. Cars blasted their horns at me, but I didn't care! It was like we were both alone in the world.

When the bus turned a corner, I stopped. I felt winded but light-headed. So this was what it felt like to be on top of the world! My lungs felt like bursting as I struggled to walk home. My shirt was drenched in sweat and my calves burned from the sprint. But I couldn't care less. My finger trailed the bruise she had touched. I grinned all the way home like an idiot.

Ariel

Something really nice happened today.

I was worried when Lasso didn't show up at my rehearsal. But Ayush did. And I was really glad it was him, and not Lasso. He waited for me till after my practice. I was in such a hurry that I just put on whatever I had grabbed from the flat before I left. It was an old T-shirt and a really worn-out pair of jeans. But he didn't seem to mind.

When we got to the bus stop, I was almost afraid that the bus would arrive too soon. We started talking and I was really surprised to hear that we like the same books and movies.

Ayush seemed really into the conversation. I started counting every bus that showed up. I missed seven, and he didn't even realise it. But I was happy to sit and just listen to him talk. When the last bus came, I had to leave. I felt really shy when he grabbed my hand and stared into my eyes. I think I blushed! I was sooooo afraid that people on the bus would think we were trying to kiss!

When I got on the bus, I thought I heard my name. Imagine my surprise when I looked out of the window and saw Ayush running after the bus!

My first reaction was that I had left something behind! I was so afraid that I poked my head out of the window. But no, it was just Ayush trying to beat the bus to the traffic junction.

The silly boy! How could he be a match for the bus? But I yelled to him, cheering him on. He must have run for about two hundred metres before he stopped.

I grinned like an idiot as I collapsed into my seat. I was still rubbing my hand, in the very same spot where he had grabbed me. I don't think I'll ever wash my hand!

13
Sucker Punched and Dunked

It was a few weeks before I saw Lasso again. He still had his arm in a cast. His father had got his braces replaced with a new set of removable ones. Apart from a faint yellow mark on his cheek, he looked fine. He was in high spirits as he recited line for line what he had memorised from *Mr Humphry's Book of Love Secrets*, the "*Six Habits of Courting Behaviour*".

1. *Before you start, check your breath. Breathe on a piece of mirror and smell the expelled breath.*
2. *Dress smartly.*
3. *Stand tall. Be confident. Do not slouch as it gives the impression that you are a weakling.*
4. *Flirting starts when you see someone you like and catch her eye. Smile. If she indicates a friendly bearing, step forward and introduce yourself.*
5. *Think of something sincere to say. If the girl senses that you are honest, she will warm up to you.*
6. *Engage and listen. Do not dominate the conversation. Let her talk and you listen!*

He passed me a little black notebook to read. He had copied everything neatly. I was impressed with his diligence. I took a pen and wrote an extra line for dramatic effect, "And do not spit, fart, scratch your balls or pick your nose!" We laughed and slapped each other on the back.

School was over and we were making our way to the bicycle shed to get our bikes. We didn't see Edward and his cronies trailing us. When we reached the shed, we felt strong arms push us from behind. I whirled around and fended off one of the boys. But they were faster and gripped me in a tight arm lock. Edward held on to Lasso's injured arm.

He looked at me warningly, "Keep quiet or I'd break this again."

I stared at him furiously. I could see Lasso whimpering in fear.

His cronies dragged us to an unused toilet at the back of the schoolyard. I looked around hoping to get help but no one was around at that time. We were pushed into the centre of the toilet and made to squat. The five boys spread out around us in a ring. Edward stood smirking. I saw with satisfaction his bandaged nose. He looked like a proboscis monkey.

I just had to say sarcastically, "I'm sorry, did I break your nose?"

He muttered a swear word and signalled to his cronies to grab us.

I saw one taking his time to approach me. I waited. When he got within three feet, I sprang up and sucker punched him. That threw him off. I made a dash for the exit, but Lasso's cry halted me.

"Ayush, save me!" he screamed.

I turned and saw Edward and three of the boys stripping Lasso. They tore off his shirt, then his trousers. They were getting to his underwear when I jumped on one of them. I pulled him off Lasso.

Just then, I felt something hard hit me on the back of my head. I slipped. When I turned around, I saw that the fifth boy was holding a pail in his hands. A freaking pail! He had used the hardest part of the pail, its bottom rim, to hit me.

Before I could react, two of the boys had pounced on me. I had my shirt and trousers removed forcibly. Then, a momentary silence before I heard one of them say quietly, "Boss, come look at this."

I felt a cold chill, and it wasn't from being almost naked. I lay on the cool ground and felt calm even though my hands and legs were pinned tight to the ground.

Edward walked over to look at my back. He said just one word, "Shit."

I almost laughed when I saw Lasso getting up naked. Even he was curious enough to limp over to peek at my back. I could imagine all six of them, jaws wide apart, gawking at my tattooed back.

"Touch me and I'll get my gang to beat you up," I said in the most ominous voice I could muster.

Edward walked around to study my face. He took a long time before laughing out loud.

"You're so full of shit, *Aron*!" he said mockingly. So he was calling my bluff. But I knew he was uncertain of my threat, because he allowed me to keep my underwear on.

I felt sick when Lasso was hauled into one of the cubicles. After five of them took turns to pee, they dunked his head in the urinal. I could just imagine how badly he wanted to scream, but I didn't hear a squeak from him at all. He was probably smart enough to keep his eyes and mouth tightly closed.

They counted to ten, laughing and screaming with glee. Next, I heard the flush. This time Lasso screamed, sputtering and coughing as his mouth filled up with water.

When they were through with him, he sobbed hysterically and wiped his face frantically against the plaster of his arm cast. I felt so angry and sorry for him! When it was my turn, Edward looked at me again. This time, he chickened out. He shrugged and signalled for his cronies to follow him.

"Next time, we will tie you to a goal post and do free kicks. Stay out of my sight," he warned.

When they were gone, I ran to help Lasso. I took his discarded shirt and wet it under a running tap. I wiped his head, hair, face, neck and shoulders the best I could. He cried so hard that by the time I was done, he had slobbered all over me. I was almost as wet and smelled just as bad. I gritted my teeth and held him.

It was the one secret that I had been trying to keep under wraps, but now my past was blown. *The entire school is going to think that I am a secret society member.*

When Lasso recovered, he shoved me aside roughly. He got onto his feet and put on his clothes, struggling with just one good arm. But I knew better than to offer help. He needed the little that was left of his pride. I looked away to save him face.

Just before he stepped out of the toilet, he had this to say, "You freak. I wished they got you too."

I was hurt to hear that from him, but I could understand how he felt. At that moment, I was glad that my tattoo had saved me from a royal flush.

When I got home that evening, my mother was cleaning the house. She took one look at my face and threw the rag she was holding at me. I ducked. It hit me on the shoulder.

"You got into a fight again! What are you trying to do, get expelled?" she screamed.

I averted my eyes when I shouted back at her. "I had an accident at the basketball court!"

"You always say that!" she yelled.

I ran to the bathroom and tore off my clothes frantically. I scrubbed myself hard, washing off every smear of pee. I looked at the mirror over the sink. I was in a sorry state. I had a bruise on my chin that had turned a sickening yellow. There were dark rings under my hollow eyes. I hesitated before turning my back, and sighed heavily when I saw the phoenix with its unleashed claws. It was such a stupid thing to do.

I was eleven when I let friends from my basketball gang talk me into getting a tattoo done. It was so bloody painful! When I felt the first prick of the machine crawling on my skin, I almost screamed and wanted to stop the tattoo artist. But with four pairs of eyes watching me, I was too proud to stop him.

It took an unbearable forty-five minutes before the first session was done. By then, I was totally drenched in sweat. I had gripped and rubbed against the chair I was sitting on so hard that the skin of my palms blistered.

When I got home, I realised I had peed in my trousers. I couldn't bear the touch of cloth against my back for almost a week! But it was my mother's reaction that really threw me off. She ranted and screamed, and smashed things in the house. She tried to cane me but I dodged her and fled.

I spent one week hiding and sleeping in different void decks. I had to, as there were seven sessions to have the tattoo imprinted. It was so painful and unbearable every time. But I couldn't chicken out as my buddies watched me like a hawk at these sessions. Every one of them had got their tattoo done; I was the last one in the group.

By the time my mother located me, she was a broken wreck. Looking gaunt and frail, she said she hadn't slept for a week. I felt really bad when she sobbed. Although I felt sorry, I didn't say anything to her. The tattoo was like a permanent mark of my independence, an imprint of identity that allowed me to stand alongside my friends.

Mum said she would take me to a doctor to have the tattoo removed, but the cost of it stopped her. It would have cost her almost two months of her salary. I convinced her that she should save the money. Very reluctantly, she agreed.

I stopped walking around bare-bodied in the flat. Seeing my tattooed back made her upset. It is something that I will have to bear with, until I am old enough to work and save money to have it removed.

I had been so careful not to have my back exposed at school. Now Edward and his cronies were probably going to use my secret against me. For once, I was really scared. Getting expelled from the Institute would kill my mother.

Lasso

I thought having my arm broken was the worst thing that could have happened to me. No, being bullied and dunked in urine definitely topped that. Nothing could have prepared me for what happened today, not even years of shitting in a hole in the ground back in the Philippines. Sucking in vile whiffs of dried shit that had accumulated over the years was nothing compared with having your head immersed in urine. It was absolutely, gut-wrenchingly revolting.

Although I had my eyes and mouth shut tight, I couldn't stop the sickening smell from seeping through my nostrils. I held my breath for as long as I could; any second longer, I would have been forced to drink my own urine.

Damn it! I blame Ayush for getting me into this shit! He was obviously their target! Why did he have to piss Edward off! And that tattoo! All this time I thought he was my friend, but he didn't even trust me enough to tell me about his past. I really, really hate him now. But I will have my revenge. I will not allow those bullies to get away.

14
Betrayal

Two days later, I was in trouble again. When the teacher called out my name during Mathematics class, I knew I had to face the music. I looked at the teacher's face, trying to guess why I had to see the principal, but he avoided looking at me.

When I passed Lasso's classroom two doors away, I wasn't surprised when I saw him coming out to join me. He walked ahead and tried to ignore me. But when he neared the principal's office, he changed his mind and said to me quietly, "Just tell the truth."

I was puzzled, but I didn't ask any questions.

Edward was waiting outside the principal's office with his four cronies. Everyone was looking down at the floor. I could tell from their posture that they were worried and maybe even scared. I felt glad I wasn't alone.

Six of us waited outside the office till the office attendant called us in. We stood facing the principal's desk; it was a tight squeeze in his small office. It didn't help that the air-conditioning was turned off. We started perspiring and the stench from somebody's body odour became unbearable. For some reason, I felt nauseous. The principal was held up elsewhere and we were kept standing. Forget about courtesy or being offered a drink; we would be lucky if we got out alive.

After what seemed like an hour, I couldn't take it any longer. The anxiety and the stench forced me running from the room. I ran past the office attendant outside the principal's office. He yelled, "Hey, you!", but I ignored him.

I got to the toilet and started retching. When I was done, I felt better. I made my way to the sink, and froze when I saw Edward leaning against a pillar, watching me.

He had a dark look on his face. Finally, he opened his mouth. "Don't say anything if you want to keep your secret. You know you will get expelled for being a secret society member."

I said nothing. I watched him walk out of the toilet. After rinsing my mouth, I made my way back to the principal's office.

I knocked on the door timidly and joined the other boys in the room. It seemed that Edward had been excused.

He wasn't with the others. When the principal looked at me, I almost collapsed.

"Is it true that these boys held Lasso and dunked his head in a toilet bowl of urine?" he asked in a serious tone.

I looked at every one of the four bullies' faces. They tried to look impassive, but their quivering hands gave them away. I turned to look at Lasso last before facing the principal. Lasso was staring at a painting of a majestic eagle flying over a green plain. The words below seemed to mock me. It read, "Honesty, Integrity, Respect".

Lasso tried to ignore me, but I could see his body language willing me to tell the truth. Edward's warning came back to taunt me. I knew he would carry out his threat and expose my secret.

I swallowed a lump in my throat. I heard my voice croak when I finally opened my mouth, "I didn't see anything, Sir."

Lasso turned to me. He looked at me furiously. He opened his mouth to protest, and then stopped himself.

"Nothing?" the principal asked again. I nodded regretfully.

I saw the look of hurt in Lasso's eyes as he turned away from me.

I looked up at the four bullies' faces. They were smirking.

When the principal dismissed us from his room, I almost wanted to run back and blurt out the truth. But I saw Edward waiting outside. He had known that I wouldn't squeal, and now, he had a gloating look on his face. I left him and his cronies nudging one another and slapping high fives.

I looked around frantically, trying to find Lasso. I finally saw him making his way back to his classroom. I ran up and reached out to touch his shoulder. Lasso whirled around and knocked my hand off angrily. His face was a blotchy red and his eyebrows were pulled taut. I had never seen him so enraged before.

He squinted at me with a mix of hatred and pity.

"You're not just a freak, you're also a coward."

I let him walk away. I had never felt smaller in my life.

—

Things got worse after our confrontation with the principal. A couple of days later, the school's website was defaced with pictures of Lasso in a green-and-purple sequined bra. I knew who had done it, of course. It was the tormentor's revenge for getting reported to the principal.

Lasso got permission to stay away from school for a week. I found out from his classmates that he had chicken pox, but I didn't try calling him.

Meanwhile, Edward kept his promise. He didn't tell anyone else in school about my tattoo. My secret was safe, for the time being.

But nothing could describe the sick, empty feeling I had in me. Lasso had tried to get the bully to face the consequences of his action. But I had betrayed him, all because I was too weak to do the right thing.

15
Humiliated at Raffles Hotel

Imagine my surprise when I received a call from Ariel, asking me to meet her at Raffles Hotel after school.

I made my way to Beach Road, where the hotel had stood for the last one hundred and ten years. I took the MRT to City Hall station, and then crossed over from Bras Basah Road. When I walked past Ah Teng's Bakery, the smells of vanilla and chocolate overwhelmed me. I also caught a whiff of curry puffs being baked. I would have given anything to wolf down even a plain bread roll! I was famished!

I was approached by a maître d' in a white starched uniform. He had a gleaming brass plate bearing his name. It shone at me ominously.

I peeped behind him at scores of well-heeled diners seated in The Tiffin Room. I felt totally out of place, and hugely embarrassed. I had hastily pulled a T over my school uniform. It smelled bad from being stuffed in my bag for at least a week. I couldn't remember if it was something I had worn home after basketball practice. I was in my school trousers. And I wasn't wearing socks.

The man gave me a look. I ignored his disapproving face.

"Are you lost?" he asked.

"Huh? I'm meeting a friend here," I said, trying hard to sound all grown-up.

Before he could dismiss me, I heard my name being called. Ariel rushed out of the restaurant, looking pleased to see me. She was still in her school uniform; her pale blue pinafore looked clean and pressed. How could she possibly look so good dressed as a schoolgirl?

Seeing her, all my feelings of insecurity vanished. Ariel made a face at the maître d' and dragged me into the restaurant.

"Just ignore him, he's a snob. I'll get my father to dock his pay if he says anything nasty!" she whispered.

I felt uneasy. So Ariel's father worked in the hotel and she was sneaking an under-dressed friend into one of his restaurants to eat.

Ariel led me to a table at the back of the restaurant. I had to walk past ten tables of smartly dressed business executives and richly attired hotel guests. Every one of them stopped talking midway to peer in my direction. I wished the ground would swallow me up. Not only did I feel impoverished, but I was also clearly way out of my league walking beside Ariel.

I tried to make myself as inconspicuous as possible. I settled in a seat facing an enormous pillar. But I was so nervous that when I shifted my butt, I heard an involuntary loud fart.

I saw Ariel stifling a giggle. I had already broken three rules in Mr Humphry's book. I had not showered, I was inappropriately dressed, and I had farted. Great.

I pretended everything was cool. I took a quick glance at the menu. Nothing was priced below $25. I probably had about $5.75 on me only. I swallowed my saliva and took a sip of cold water from a glass.

"Ariel."

I heard a voice. No, it couldn't be.

I turned around and saw Lasso standing behind me. He was no longer wearing his cast. And he was dressed smartly in a short-sleeved shirt and a tie. A freaking tie! He even had time to change into a pair of jeans! He must have gone home, showered and rushed over.

I looked at him. He seemed... different! I stared hard at his stomach. Somehow, he managed to look thin. What did he do, put on a girdle? And his hair, it was combed for a change. In fact, everything about him looked polished! Wow. What a dramatic transformation. He must have memorised every courting principle in *Mr Humphry's Book of Love Secrets*!

Lasso returned my enquiring look like he was going to crush a cockroach. I saw him glance briefly at my crumpled, stinky shirt. Because he refrained from saying anything rude, I decided not to tease him about his flattened stomach either.

Grabbing a seat beside Ariel, he waved to a waiter and picked up a menu. He settled on a plate of sausages and mashed potatoes. Ariel chose the fish and chips. Then they both looked at me.

"I'm not hungry," I said. My stomach growled in protest. I hoped they didn't hear that.

Lasso couldn't care less. He placed their orders and started chatting with Ariel. He was complaining about his recent bout of chicken pox. I looked at his face curiously; I didn't believe him, of course. His skin was as smooth as a baby's backside! There were no scabs or any evidence of a breakout. Ariel listened politely, occasionally looking across at me with a smile. I kept drinking the cold water.

Bored, I looked out of the window. I smiled when I recognised the flowers. The well-groomed lawn boasted spreads of yellow frangipani blooms, lush red heliconias and pink and red ginger torch blossoms. I knew their names as the last two flowers were the same ones Mum had grown along the corridor of our flat.

As a very young boy, I loved sitting outside our flat, watching Mum tend to her plants. I remembered thinking she was so pretty! She was tall and had long shapely legs. She always had a quiet feminine air about her, very regal-like.

When I was slightly older, I understood that we were different from other people. I had no father. I imagined that my mother was a queen who had been banished from her kingdom because she had made someone angry. I wanted so badly for my mother to be of royal blood; that would have made my father a king, and me, a prince.

When the food arrived, I snapped out of my daydream. I looked on hungrily as Lasso and Ariel picked the exact pair of fork and knife to use. I was glad I wasn't eating; I was confused with the spread of cutlery in front of me. Mum had never taken me out to a fine-dining place. We couldn't afford it.

I was surprised when Ariel handed me a small plate of deep fried cod and some fries. She knew. I looked at it, my stomach growling. I nodded gratefully at her.

I sneaked a look to see which fork she was using. I picked a replica on my end and tucked into my food.

Ariel talked only about her drama rehearsals. I could see she was really excited about the upcoming show. Lasso didn't say much while eating. Aside from having whined about his chicken pox, he treated me like I was invisible.

When the bill came, I wasn't surprised to see Lasso whipping out his debit card. But Ariel told him her father would foot the bill. We left our table with Lasso and Ariel walking ahead of me. The restaurant was less crowded by then, but people still looked when I passed them. I swore to myself that it would be the first and last time I stepped into a place where a lady had to hold her nose when I got too close.

ARIEL

Our exams had kept us busy studying for weeks! Rehearsals for the play had been cut back so I had no reason to see Lasso, or Ayush. I was very anxious to meet Ayush, so I decided to call him. I told him to join me at my father's restaurant. That way, I could eat without having to pay for my meal. Dad's always happy to pay for my friends too.

But I think I shouldn't have asked Lasso along. Ayush didn't seem happy to see him, and neither was Lasso happy to see Ayush. There was some tension between them, but I couldn't tell what it was. I felt a little hurt when Ayush said he wasn't hungry when it came to ordering. But when my food came, I felt it was only polite to offer him some. After all, I was the one who had asked him out.

He seemed quiet and not quite himself today. I stole glances at him a couple of times. I don't think he even realised it. Lasso, as always, was clueless about the situation. He was pretty quiet too.

Maybe I shouldn't have invited Ayush to my dad's restaurant. I hope he didn't think I was trying to show off. I think about him all the time. I just wanted to see him.

Lasso

Today confirmed a lingering suspicion I had about Ayush. I was really surprised to see him at the hotel. I hadn't expected Ariel to invite him for lunch. I had waited so long to see her!

It made me feel good to see him so out of place. I kind of felt sorry for him when I saw people looking disapprovingly in his direction. I knew he was trying to act nonchalant, but it was tough. I can imagine how embarrassed I'd be if a woman held her nose when I got close! Oh man, how could Ariel possibly tolerate that body odour! And really, what was he thinking of? All those times reading *Mr Humphry's Book of Love Secrets*, didn't he learn anything? He should have showered at least!

But I'm happy he was so sloppy. He must have looked really bad when I stood beside him. Surely Ariel must have realised that I looked more presentable? I always knew he had a soft spot for Ariel! I could have killed him when he took her portion of fried cod and fries. I was starving! My own plate of sausages and mashed potatoes was hardly enough! But I knew better than to eat too much in front of Ariel. She's always whining about how much I pig out. Today, I controlled myself, thanks to Ayush's presence.

When I got home, I couldn't stop bingeing. At the last count, I had eaten five packs of potato chips, two cups of instant noodles and I'm on to my third bar of Snickers chocolate now. But I'm still hungry.

16
A History Lesson

I read *Mr Humphry's Book of Love Secrets* again before I went to bed. It must have been the fourteenth time I had read the book since I laid my hands on it. I had stolen it to help Lasso. But it looked like I needed the book more than he did now.

I couldn't believe how inadequate I had felt in The Tiffin Room. Should I be surprised? Both Lasso and Ariel are clearly from a better family background. I wished I could be angry with her for inviting me to the hotel, but I just couldn't. She had been so sweet in sharing her food with me. She probably thought that I would have enjoyed eating at a posh restaurant. She couldn't have been more wrong.

I remembered reading about Raffles Hotel in one of my history books. It was one of many institutions named after the founder of Singapore. The only thing I remembered from the account was that the hotel saw one of the last few tigers in Singapore killed on its premises, way back in 1902!

A runaway tiger from a circus had found its way under a table in the Bar & Billiard Room. It had taken a marksman, an Englishman no less, to shoot the tiger.

What I felt in The Tiffin Room was probably close to what the tiger had felt for being shot – a bruised ego. Despite the humiliation, the grandeur of the hotel wasn't lost on me.

I saw pictures of the hotel's British past when I walked along its corridors. It smacked of opulence, of a time when Singapore's British colonial masters rolled their tongue when they spoke.

To see social habits that have been passed down, we don't have to look too far really. Drinking tea and ballroom dancing – these are the things Mum enjoys.

It was also the British who introduced most of the sports that we play today. Sports like horse-racing, boat-racing, cricket and golf were common before 1900. Then there are sports like badminton, football, rugby and hockey, which were played in the early twentieth century.

Thomas S.R. Institute remains a leading contender in cricket matches among schoolboys. It is played largely by Indians. I know many boys talk behind my back in school. They wonder about my mixed ancestry. Am I Indian, since my name is Ayush?

It always amuses me when I shock people the moment I speak Mandarin. I was the top student in Chinese in my primary school, even though my father was Indian. I had guessed his race from the time I was old enough to notice that my deep-set eyes and sharp features were different from my mum's. I never dared to ask her more than what she was willing to reveal, as I didn't want to feel guilty when she got upset. But I like to think that she was in love with my father. Her choice in staying single makes me believe that.

I wondered if *Mr Humphry's Book of Love Secrets* was placed by a teacher to show what people were reading back in the nineteenth century, or was it a prank played by a lovesick schoolboy? Whatever it was, I was grateful to have found the book. It was helping me make sense of my confused feelings. And I didn't feel like a freak anymore for having the recurring nightmare of Ariel as a naked mermaid. I realised too that I needed to groom myself if I hoped to feel confident walking beside her.

Interestingly, when the book was first published in 1891 in the United Kingdom, over in North America, basketball was invented by a Canadian man named Dr James Naismith. His game was created in answer to a harsh winter barring outdoor play.

Mr Humphry, you were obviously a fine, dandy gentleman who preferred scoring in courtship. You probably knew which fork and knife to use when dining, or what to say in the company of women. Your book will help me to learn how to behave around a girl. As for Dr Naismith, because of your invention, I have a source of pride. When I play basketball, the boys in the Institute forget that I'm from a different social class. All that matters is that I'm really good at it.

17
Nightmare from Fight Club

I didn't see Lasso around school. He had dropped out of basketball. I didn't even get a chance to ask him about the bra pictures. The school had been quick to remove the pictures just as quickly as the hacker had put them up on the website.

Edward left me mostly alone during practice. But more than once, I caught him watching me play with a grudging look on his face. I tried to guess what he was thinking. Was it jealousy or admiration? Once, to my surprise, Edward actually clapped after I buried a three pointer. I turned to him and took a long look. All my years of playing with street kids surfaced when I saw the knowing look he threw my way. It said, "Watch out. I'm going to get you."

Two days later, Edward waited for me outside school. It was a deserted space near a multi-storey car park. He had his cronies and a couple of new "friends" with him. I recognised one of them immediately. It was Shawn, from my Fight Club days. His slicked-back hair reflected the glare of the afternoon sun.

I knew he remembered me when he asked, "Where's Mama?"

I did a silent headcount. There were nine of them. There was no way I was going to get away. I decided to fake my bravado.

"You know him?" I nodded in Edward's direction.

"He had been looking for me for weeks! Rumour has it that someone in your school is claiming to be one of my gang members," Shawn said.

I almost choked on my saliva. Before I could say anything, Shawn indicated to one of his followers to step forward. The man lifted his shirt and revealed a massive tattoo on his chest. Then he turned slowly and showed us a second tattoo.

"Is it the same picture?" Shawn asked, looking bored.

Edward looked hard at me. "You lied, *Aron*," he jeered.

Shawn looked at me, and then turned to Edward. "He still fights?" he asked about me.

One of Edward's cronies broke in eagerly. "He's got a powerful kick!"

Edward silenced him with an angry, embarrassed look. Shawn saw his shame and laughed heartily.

"So what? You asked me to confirm if he's one of my gang, he's NOT!" Shawn said.

Edward shrugged, unsure of what to say.

"What do you do to liars?" Shawn asked again.

This time, Edward had an answer. He said gloatingly, "The royal flush. Same treatment as boys who report us to the principal."

Shawn took a moment to think. Then he said to me, "Chindian. I've seen you fight. You must be very good still, if this boy wants to expose you."

Shawn stopped to light a cigarette. He took a few puffs, seeming to think of a solution.

"Tell you what. Come join me. I will protect you. No one will dare to bully you," he finally suggested.

I felt a crushing feeling in the chest. I couldn't breathe! The pressure of it. I wished I hadn't antagonised Edward. Shawn expected me to join his gang? How the hell was I going to get myself out of this shit?

I stalled for time. Shawn finished his cigarette and flicked the butt away. He reached for his cigarette box, cursing loudly when he saw that it was empty. Then, without warning, he hurled the box at me. I dodged on instinct, the box just missing my ear by inches. Shawn was pleased with my quick reflex.

He grinned, "I need someone like you. Don't turn me down."

He turned to leave. His followers gathered behind him. I could make out a plastic orange comb sticking out of Shawn's back trouser pocket. How typical of an *Ah Beng*. Then I saw the outline of a bigger object tucked under the shirt of one of the men. It looked suspiciously like the kitchen chopper Mum used to mince meat. I felt huge sweat stains gather under my armpits. The heat from the sun burned into the back of my neck.

"Show him the cat you caught," Shawn said in an amused tone. One of the men disappeared into a stairwell in the multi-storey car park. What he dragged out took me by surprise. It was a boy from our school, still dressed in his uniform. I recognised him immediately. It was Lasso! He was blindfolded and had a rope bound around his wrists. He was barely conscious.

I didn't let on that I knew him. I saw Edward watching Lasso with guilt and uncertainty written all over his face. He hadn't known about Lasso being in their hands either.

He turned and looked at me for help. Clearly, this wasn't something he had expected.

An old image of Lasso drenched in urine came up in my head.

Shawn indicated for one of his gangsters to punch Lasso. Before the man could lay a finger, I yelled furiously at him, "OK!"

Edward whipped around and looked at me in shock.

"You idiot! You're going to get expelled for joining their gang!" he hissed at me angrily.

I shot back an angry retort, "You stupid fool! What did you get us into? They have knives on them!"

A flicker of terror crossed Edward's eyes. This time, he realised that he had gone too far. What a jerk! Involving the secret society? What a stupid thing to do!

I had the absolute satisfaction when I saw Edward's lips start to quiver. Then it was my time to gloat when Shawn shouted over his shoulder, "Tell me if anyone bullies you in school. Let the fat kid go!"

Edward stepped away from me immediately. He signalled to his cronies and, together, they walked away hurriedly.

Shawn's last warning came loud and clear. "And if anyone reports us to the principal, we'll just crush his balls!"

Shawn's men left Lasso lying on the ground. Then they left.

I rushed to Lasso's side and crouched beside him. I slapped him on the cheek a couple of times, and then he came to. I removed his blindfold and rope. When he got more clear-headed, he moaned.

"Someone grabbed me and hit me," he whined pathetically. I nodded and helped him to sit up.

"Was it you? You're so full of shit!" he croaked hoarsely.

I felt like punching him. I had just saved him and he thought I had set him up.

I shoved him hard in the chest and got up. I walked away quickly. His voice was still ringing long after I left him. "You'd better hope I don't tell my father! He's going to beat the crap out of you!"

18

Sleepless Night

That night, I took out my punching bag from the bottom of my cupboard. It was dusty; the leather had turned a mouldy white. Mum had forbidden me to touch it after I started school at the Institute.

"Focus on your basketball," she had pleaded. I had agreed as I was relieved I could start life afresh. No one knew me and I assumed that my checkered past would remain a secret.

The punching bag was something Mum bought me. After the incident at the playground, she came home with a punching bag. She set it up and had it attached to a metal ring she drilled into the ceiling. She told me to punch into it every time I felt angry or frustrated. She even taught me a few boxing moves from researching on the Internet.

She figured out how to make the right fist and throw basic punches: the jab, the straight right, the uppercut. She even taught me how to box while standing correctly, feet not too far apart, left foot placed fifteen inches ahead of the right.

I felt some of the punches come naturally. I must have been born with an instinct to defend myself. Every time I punched, the bag would swing back at me. I imagined the face of a bully as I dodged, then I rounded my fist, thumb aligned with my folded fingers, and aimed straight for a "nose".

I chuckled when I recalled the day I sucker punched Edward. Even though I was furious with him, I had restrained myself. I could have broken his nose, but I gave him just a broken capillary.

I had YouTube to thank for my continued interest in learning to defend myself. I watched clips of famous boxing legends. Like Muhammad Ali. I even emulated the slacked-jaw oomph of Sylvester Stallone in *Rocky* when he connected a punch. And when Mum told me about Bruce Lee, I learnt to develop a cross-combination of short stab boxing and flying kick.

On Saturdays, Mum would take on part-time work for extra money. That was when I would spend all my time trying out different moves. I had read that serious boxers kept to a strict regime of "The Three Hundred" – a hundred push-ups, a hundred sit-ups, fifty pull-ups and fifty minutes of running. It took me almost nine months before I could handle "The Three Hundred" comfortably. I relied on my training to protect me from the likes of Edward. I built body mass and confidence. The bullies naturally stopped picking on me. And the name-calling ceased as well.

But getting into Fight Club must have been one of the dumbest things to do. The unresolved fight with Shawn probably provoked his decision to recruit me. I didn't believe his intention was to protect me from bullies in school. The dreadful things I knew he was capable of would soon rear their heads. I had to find a way to keep this a secret from Mum. If she found out that I had joined Shawn and his gang, she'd probably skin me alive with her kitchen chopper.

—

That night I dreamt of Ariel again. I found myself in an open space. I heard a moan. It became louder. I heard whimpering next. I followed the sounds and came to a huge tree.

Then I saw her. She was bound with rope on the other side of the tree. I could make out the side of her back and her long, flowing hair. I heard her gasp. I ran towards her and saw Shawn crouching at her feet! Then I looked closer and saw that it wasn't her feet, but her tail!

Shawn looked up and grinned menacingly at me. He stretched himself and pressed against Ariel. I could see his body crush against Ariel's chest. He leaned in towards her and sniffed at her neck. His tongue stuck out and touched the skin of her throat.

"No!" I yelled, but no sound emitted from my mouth.

I lunged forward and grabbed him by the shoulder. I spun him around and balled up my fists. But he just leered into my face. Then he raised a knife towards me...

I woke up with a jolt. I was drenched in sweat. I looked around me – I was in bed. I clutched my face hard, I was so angry! I had never felt more helpless! What had I got myself into!

19
An Unusual Science Lesson

During a combined Science lesson with Lasso's class, we had a review of the human respiratory system. The topic was to understand how the human body took in oxygen. When we had to do an in-depth study of the trachea, diaphragm and the lungs, the teacher took out a human model to show how the breath of life passed through the body.

"Who wants to have a go at CPR?" the teacher asked. I was amused when Lasso put up his hand eagerly.

Lasso was told to get down on his knees beside the model. He was guided to use his fingers to locate its upper rib cage, and then place his hands on top of each other over the sternum. He did ten chest compressions before the teacher stopped him.

He couldn't wait to get to the next step. Quickly, he leant forward and sealed his mouth over the model. He breathed out and tilted his head to watch the chest rise. He did a more dramatic mouth-blowing the second time. And a third.

Then something went wrong. He couldn't seem to lift his mouth! He collapsed and sprawled on the ground, arms flailing wildly. His mouth was still locked with the model's, and he made weird strangled noises like "uumph" and "errghh". The boys looked around at one another and started sniggering. Was he playing the fool?

"That's enough! Get off!" the teacher barked fiercely.

But Lasso didn't budge. Finally, he let out a mangled screech. The boys started laughing. I stood up in my seat anxiously to peer at him. The teacher got really flustered and tried to yank Lasso off the model, which resulted in even more muffled screaming. Then someone yelled, "Blood!"

I was horrified when I saw a trickle of blood flowing down the cheek of the model. I ran forward hurriedly. Getting down on my knees, I slipped a finger between their mouths. Lasso's braces had got caught in the rubber. I didn't know what to do.

Then I recalled an image of Lasso's loosened braces in a bloodied mess when he was injured at the basketball court. I got up and yelled for Vaseline. I knew one of the boys in class always carried it on him. I smeared some on my finger and ran back to Lasso. By then, everyone in class had gathered around him to watch the ordeal.

I slipped my lubricated finger into Lasso's mouth. I was just able to feel the clasps that held his braces. I pushed them off his teeth, thanks to the Vaseline. As soon as the braces were released, Lasso was able to lift one cheek. He then stuck his finger in his mouth and ejected the offending items. Now he looked like a vampire with blood smeared around his lips.

The boys laughed and cheered! Lasso turned pink in the face. But being a good sport, he just smiled gallantly.

"What were you trying to do? Kiss it awake?" one boy asked.

Someone yelled, "He thinks he's Prince Charming!"

More guffaws. I took out a handkerchief and passed it to Lasso. He took it gratefully and wiped his mouth tenderly. Then he picked up his braces and wrapped them in the handkerchief. The teacher looked cross at having been upstaged. He dismissed the class when the bell rang. But as Lasso slipped out of the room, I saw that the teacher couldn't stop chuckling to himself.

When I went out, Lasso was waiting for me. I gave him a small nod.

"I shouldn't have stuck my tongue in," he said with a twinkle in his eye.

I laughed out loud. *Mr Humphry's Book of Love Secrets*, Chapter 22, *"The Art of French Kissing"*.

Lasso turned serious. He looked at me and said, "I heard from one of Edward's friends that you saved me from the gangsters."

I looked away and nodded.

"Thanks," Lasso said humbly. "Sorry I accused you of grabbing me."

I looked him in the eye. "It's ok. Not the first time I've been accused of something that I didn't do. I'm used to it."

As we walked off, Lasso put an arm around my back. After a beat, he asked, "Friends again?"

I didn't answer him immediately. He had no idea how I was feeling. I was terribly jealous. Had he kissed Ariel? A horrid, twisted feeling shot through me like a sharp jab. Better not go there. It wasn't like I had any other friends in school. I managed a lop-sided grin at him in reply.

20
Three's Company

When it is time for the prince to get married, he picks a princess from a neighbouring kingdom. The little mermaid is heartbroken. Her sisters approach the old sea witch and trade their beautiful hair for a knife. If the little mermaid can draw a few drops of the prince's blood with the sea witch's knife, she can turn her legs back into a fish tail...

Ariel arranged to meet me after her rehearsal. This time, I told her pointedly that I wished to avoid the Raffles Hotel. We decided on McDonald's.

I took pains to shower after school and put on a matching outfit – a white cotton shirt paired with blue jeans. I picked clean ones and even ironed them. Just before I left the flat, I borrowed one of Mum's deodorants to rub liberally on the soles of my feet. What she didn't see wouldn't hurt.

As I walked down the stairs, I exhaled into my palm just to check my breath. All clear. I had flossed and brushed my teeth thoroughly – twice.

When I reached Takashimaya Shopping Centre, I checked the time. It was still early. I waited patiently outside McDonald's. I was excited about seeing Ariel. This time, I was dressed right. I felt good and confident too.

Imagine my disappointment when I saw her walking in with Lasso ten minutes later. She even had her right arm hooked over his elbow. I felt hurt and confused. When she saw me, she seemed to read my mood immediately. She withdrew her arm hurriedly and gave me an apologetic grin.

Lasso didn't seem surprised to see me. So he knew Ariel had arranged to meet me.

Over a meal of hamburgers and fries, they talked about Shakespeare. I was bored with their conversation and didn't join in. I let my mind drift and started studying the people around us.

Then I saw him. It was Shawn, with two of his men. He was browsing in a watch shop. There was something odd about his behaviour. He seemed nervous and I could see him mopping his forehead with his sleeve. His two followers were lounging around metres away from him, seeming to keep a lookout.

I watched as he got near a showcase. He kept fingering its rim and fiddling with the handle. He looked around furtively several times. Finally, he removed something from his pocket. It looked like a metal object.

I sat up immediately. I saw him trying to force it through the rim of the showcase. He failed the first time.

On his second attempt, he jumped suddenly when his hand touched the metal object. He must have hurt himself as I could see him wince in pain, clutching his fist and pinning it to his crotch. He was trying his best not to scream or curse. I almost burst out laughing!

On the third try, he looked over his shoulder just once before he ran the object more confidently under the rim of the showcase. The door of the showcase gave way. I was aghast. Didn't anyone in the shop realise what he had done?

But by then, one of Shawn's followers had shielded him by standing right next to him. Shawn slipped a hand into the showcase and took out several watches. He hid a few under his shirt and stuffed several more into his trousers hurriedly.

When he tucked his metal tool into the back pocket of his trousers, I stood up, ready to yell for attention. But before I could utter a single word, I heard a piercing shriek.

It was Ariel. I looked down at the table. Floating in her cup of Coke was a pair of braces! I looked at Lasso next. His face was red with embarrassment. I laughed out loud.

"It HIT me in the FACE!" Ariel screeched and wiped her face furiously.

Lasso tried to pacify her by whipping out his handkerchief and offering to wipe her face. But she was so angry that she slapped his hand sharply.

She took another look at the braces in her Coke and started chanting "Arrgh, arrgh, arrgh" over and over again. I didn't blame her. I could see disgusting bits of food stuck in them. It was awful.

Ariel was now pink in the face. She looked so adorable and pissed that I felt like kissing her! Lasso finally fished his braces out from her cup. He switched his cup with hers, but I knew she wouldn't touch anything of his now.

"Not funny!" she yelled when Lasso tried to say something.

I stopped laughing when Lasso turned to me with a fierce glare. Ariel gathered her things and stood up to leave.

Lasso pleaded with her pitifully. "I'm sorry, they were loose! I didn't do it on purpose!" he cried desperately.

I felt like I had landed a prized catch when Ariel grabbed my arm. She pulled me out of McDonald's, leaving me barely enough time to mouth a "Sorry, got to go!"

Lasso looked ready to break down in tears. I felt sorry for him, but pleased. Round One in my favour, thanks to the shooting braces!

But as Ariel and I walked past the watch shop, a sense of foreboding came over me. I turned to look at the robbed showcase with its door hanging open. I waved madly to a salesgirl busy serving a customer at the back of the store.

When she finally realised what I was trying to tell her, she shouted for her colleagues, "Someone stole our watches!"

Ariel was oblivious to the commotion. She continued walking, dragging me with her. I could make out blood stains left on the floor near the showcase. Shawn's. I looked around me frantically, but Shawn and his two men were nowhere in sight. I was safe for now, but I felt nervous for Ariel. I put one arm around her and she smiled at me in response.

I dreaded the day he would call. I knew it'd be a matter of time before he asked me to take on my first "induction" task. I wondered what nefarious scheme he'd put me up to.

Ariel

I finally saw Ayush again today. It had been weeks since we met! My hunch about the last meal was right. He told me he didn't like going to a fancy restaurant. So I picked McDonald's this time as I only wanted to see him.

But just before I left the flat, Lasso called. When he heard I was meeting Ayush, he said he wanted to come along too. He sounded so pathetic that I relented.

Then Lasso had to go spoil it when he spat his braces into my Coke. I couldn't believe it! What did he think it was, a stupid joke? At first, when I saw his horrified face, I thought it was a genuine accident. But when Ayush smiled, I started to suspect they were playing a prank on me! I was almost positive when I saw Ayush smile at Lasso as I grabbed his arm to leave McDonald's. These boys, will they ever grow up?

Later, I was surprised when Ayush put one arm around me protectively. It felt nice. He didn't remove his arm till we left the mall. I was half hoping he would take my hand, but he didn't. His mind seemed pre-occupied with something.

Lasso

Just when I thought we were friends again, Ayush had to go spoil it all! I didn't feel angry when I saw him waiting for Ariel and me at McDonald's. I even felt happy for him when I saw that he had taken the trouble to shower and dress smart. Ariel was pleased to see him looking decent for a change. I tried to include him in our conversation after we had our burgers and fries, but he simply wasn't interested. What could possibly have got into him today? He kept looking at the watch shop outside McDonald's! If I could guess, I'd say he was secretly wishing he had money to buy himself an expensive watch. I know Ayush isn't from a well-to-do family. I'm not much better off really! My father only plays basketball for a living. Our classmates have fathers who are prominent surgeons or filthy rich businessmen! But at least I have a father, unlike Ayush. I wasn't amused when he laughed at me. How could he! I didn't ask for my braces to fall into Ariel's drink! It was an accident! I was really hurt when I saw Ariel leaving with Ayush. He could have stopped her, but he didn't! I thought I saw him smirking with glee, but I must have been wrong. He's my best friend; he wouldn't do that, would he? Ayush and I are brothers; we would never fight over a girl! It'd be really stupid to hurt our friendship because of Ariel.

21
Who's Better?

The next day outside school, I saw Lasso perching forlornly on a railing beside the monsoon drain. He was waiting for his ride home.

"Hey, where did both of you go after McDonald's?" he asked.

I chucked my bag on the ground and climbed to sit beside him. I was debating if I should tell him about Shawn, but I changed my mind.

"Nowhere. Went straight home," I replied casually.

Lasso threw me a suspicious look. What came next was totally unexpected. He did this massive coughing up of phlegm, and right before my startled eyes, brought up a huge blob of spit and shot it across the pathway. It landed about a metre from where we were perched. Wow. I was impressed.

"She's my girl. Get that into your head!" he said in a low snarl.

I didn't acknowledge him immediately. After a while, I held both palms to my mouth and coughed a few times into them to loosen my phlegm. I did a large spasm of "Ahem, ahem, ahem" and then went "Caaaa-phuuuiii!" into the air. The monstrous glob of spittle shot out of my mouth and launched itself like a torpedo across the pathway. It landed farther than Lasso's spit.

I grinned at Lasso. He looked furious! Then, the absurdity of the situation hit us. We both started laughing hard.

When the ride for him came, he jumped off the railing and turned around to face me. Then, he saluted me smartly.

"My best friend, *Spitting Extraordinaire*."

And just like that, he took off. I chuckled and made my way home.

22
Street Corner Gangs

Growing up without a father was tough. There was no male authority to discipline me. Mum tried her best, but it was hard for me to talk to her.

She didn't even understand why I sought the company of my basketball friends. Most of the boys I met at the basketball court were school dropouts. Mostly thirteen and fourteen-year-olds, studies and getting a job were the last things on their mind. Some of the older ones had got into trouble before, like for shoplifting and selling illegal VCDs.

A couple of them had tried straightening out. They had been nabbed and enrolled in a streetwise programme which had them counselled and retrained. But coming from homes where there was little attention from parents, many found themselves slipping back into their errant ways.

I enjoyed the company of these boys for the sense of belonging and security they gave me. Mum has never had a male friend in her life; she has no siblings and so I grew up without any cousins. The "Fight Club Boys", as my friends used to call themselves, were the only people who understood me.

In the past, I would turn a deaf ear when my gang mates talked about confronting arrogant bullies in school. Sure, there was the occasional fight, but we knew where to draw the line. No weapons and no kicking below the belt. Then some of them got bored with Fight Club. One day, the group decided to set up a racket to steal hand phones.

There was a lot of money involved. One of the gang leaders designed a scheme to recruit student volunteers for charity donation drives. These were genuine collection efforts made in the names of reputable charity organisations.

Over a weekend at a hawker centre, the innocent "runts", as they were called, would be made to work in pairs in their uniforms. While they approached diners for money at crowded tables, there would be a second team of runners bringing up the rear.

As soon as a donor put his money in the tin, a boy would come up from behind to pick up a $2 note from under his table. When asked if he had dropped the money, the donor would greedily accept it, although he knew it wasn't his. During the exchange when the donor was distracted, another boy would step in to remove the donor's hand phone, usually placed on the table.

The last two boys would never be in uniform. They also did not know the "runts" who were recruited for the donation jobs. I was always made the one to grab the hand phone. The gang leader felt that my calmness was an asset that could get me out of a tight situation.

We could easily steal up to twelve hand phones over a weekend. Once the SIM cards were removed, we would trawl Lucky Plaza in Orchard Road and City Plaza in Geylang to sell these hand phones to foreign workers. With the money made, we would hang out at LAN shops to play shooting games. *World of Warcraft*, *Counter Strike*, *Call of Duty*. Just name any of the top LAN games, my friends and I excelled in them.

Mum had a hunch that I was in bad company. I used to resent her incessant nagging. She begged me to quit the group countless times. Although I ignored her, I knew it in myself that I was headed for trouble.

When we were finally caught, I was so terrified! The trial in the juvenile court really freaked me out. While waiting for my hearing in the lock-up, I met other hardcore gangsters who were barely eighteen. They had been caught for rioting or possession of dangerous weapons. There was also one who was suspected of *killing* a man in a bar brawl.

My "crime" seemed small compared with theirs, but the thought of being locked up with them in the same cell made me realise how stupid I had been. I was good in my studies. I was also a star athlete in school. And I was going to throw it all away!

When I saw how upset I had made my mother, I felt really bad. I told myself that if I got out of the hearing unscathed, I would live my life straight.

23
Mischief-makers

When I showed up for basketball training, I was surprised to see almost everyone in the team huddled together in the centre of the court, poring over copies of *The New Paper*. Edward was in the group, reading out excerpts from the papers loudly.

"Look at this! Manhole covers!" he shrieked with glee. The boys burst out laughing.

"No, this is funnier...'*Pet Shop Finds Rabbits Hopping Mad Outside*!'" More laughter.

I was curious and decided to join them. No one paid any attention to me when I sat down and pulled over a copy to read. It looked like a bunch of mischief-makers had gone around town creating trouble. Some petty acts included stealing manhole covers on deserted streets and sneaking into pet shops to release animals from their enclosures.

The worst one was of a ten-year-old boy made to straddle dangerously over the parapet outside his flat, while his friends took photos for "stunt bragging". I shook my head in dismay. How could anyone find these acts funny?

When Coach showed up, everyone scrambled to hide the newspapers. I saw Edward give me a look, but he didn't say anything nasty. Come to think of it, he had given me a wide berth since the Shawn incident. I chuckled when I thought of how terrified he was that afternoon when I declared that Shawn had a weapon on him. I wouldn't be surprised if he had peed in his trousers, the wimp.

Coach made us do individual drills. Two hundred shots for a shooting drill! Oh man...it took FOREVER to get the ball in two hundred times! After that, he made us run suicide sprints. I got so disoriented running back and forth the free throw line, three-point line and half-court line that I stumbled and fell. Coach must have realised that we had had enough, and called it a day.

In the changing room, I crashed on the bench. I had never been so tired after practice before! When I recovered, I realised that Lasso hadn't been with us during training. I felt uneasy. Last night, he had texted me to tell me he would return for practice.

I stayed back after the rest had left. I went to look for Coach and found him in the staff room. He was drinking a mug of coffee. He saw me and called out.

"Ayush! Need something?" He got up and strode towards me.

He was in a pair of shorts, which was unusual. He always wore trainer pants on the court. Then I saw something I had never noticed before – a long, jagged scar along the length of his left leg. He saw me looking at it.

"Ugly, I know," he said.

I nodded my head reluctantly. "What happened?"

"Got dragged by a motorcycle, chained to the back seat," he said matter-of-factly.

My jaw dropped. He chuckled before adding, "It wasn't an accident. I was set upon by secret society gangsters."

I felt guilty immediately. The image of Shawn stealing from the watch shop surfaced in my head. I clammed up and tried to excuse myself.

Coach asked, "Where's Lasso? He said he was coming back for training."

A bigger sense of foreboding came over me. I tried to shrug off the feeling. "Maybe he's caught up at his girlfriend's drama rehearsal," I said quickly. I was surprised I could say "girlfriend" so readily.

Coach nodded his head. What he said next took me by surprise. "You're very talented, Ayush. Don't let it go to waste."

I looked at him suspiciously, willing him to explain his statement. But Coach just turned and walked back to his seat. I stepped out to leave the room.

"Don't be distracted by girls! You have a long way ahead of you!" he shouted after me.

I felt my face go red immediately. I had always known I was good at sports, but no one had complimented me so explicitly. I fled quickly.

Coach had already confirmed what I had gone to ask, that Lasso had told him he was coming back to the team. Where the hell was he?

I went to get my bike from the backyard shed. When I wheeled it out of the rack, it wobbled unsteadily. I bent to look at the tyres, and cursed when I saw a jagged tear along its front wheel.

I fingered it, puzzled. It looked like someone had sliced it with a sharp object. I looked around; the place was deserted.

I decided to push my bike home. It would be a long walk, but I could spare the time. I didn't feel like going back to an empty flat.

About fifty metres outside the school, something made me stop. I saw a bunch of boys from school gathered outside a rubbish dump at the back of an HDB block. I recognised them as Edward's cronies. They were still wearing their white trousers from school.

I tried to stride past them nonchalantly, but one of them saw me. I heard him hailing, "Ayush! Come save your boyfriend!"

I tried to ignore him and quickened my pace. Then I heard Edward's loud, arrogant voice. "Aawww, the poor fatso's crying till Mama saves him!"

Out of curiosity more than anything else, I stopped and threw my bike aside. I walked over to join them. I looked at them defiantly with fists rounded by my side. Edward saw my defensive stance and laughed shrilly.

"Relax, no one's picking a fight," he soothed mockingly.

"Who are you talking about?" I asked as calmly as I could. Even before Edward could answer, I heard his voice. Lasso's voice. The sound seemed to be coming from one of the dumpsters. I looked at Edward quizzically.

He answered my look, "We didn't do anything. We heard from someone at school that a bunch of boys had caught and dragged Lasso here. We came here only to find him gagged."

The sense of foreboding returned. I signalled for him to step aside. I watched warily as Edward and his four cronies moved aside and let me pass. I walked up to the dumpster, careful to keep them in my line of sight. Rule No. 1 in Fight Club: Never turn your back on someone you don't trust.

Still with an eye on the five of them, I shouted for Lasso before I reached the dumpster. I heard a muffled scream, "Arggh, arrgh..."

When I reached the dumpster, I put up my hands, gripped the top edge and lifted myself up. I hung half a body over the dumpster and peeped into its bottom. My hands almost lost their grip when I saw Lasso sitting at the bottom, gagged and bound.

But it wasn't the sight of him that made me slip. It was the swarm of cockroaches running around him that freaked me out. I jumped back hastily, landing my bum on the hard ground. I heard wicked laughter behind me. *Damned, now they know.*

Edward and the boys were nudging one another and rolling around laughing. I glared at them angrily.

"Come on, don't be idiots! Get him out of there!" I shouted furiously.

Edward finally stopped laughing.

"Aawww. I'm terrified of cockroaches. He's all yours!" he declared magnanimously before gathering his cronies.

After they left, I took a long time to think. By then, Lasso was totally frustrated. He must have managed to roll himself to the edge of the dumpster. He was now furiously kicking its wall!

I yelled to him, "Stop that! I'm trying to think!"

After what seemed like an eternity, I finally managed to find a discarded wooden crate. I heaved myself with some difficulty onto the edge of the dumpster again; it was harder to do it now with one hand supporting my body weight and the other holding on to a crate. I swung the crate over my head and dropped it on the opposite side of where Lasso was lying. Then I swung over the edge, and landed right on top of the crate.

I stood there for some time, watching the horde of cockroaches scuttling about. How did they get in here? *I'll kill whoever it was that set this up.*

I was debating how I was going to get to Lasso when he finally managed to release the cloth gagging his mouth. He screamed an obscenity at me, cursing and swearing at me for taking so long.

"You idiot! Hurry up! There are insects crawling all over me!"

I shouted right back at him, "How the hell did you get into THIS SHIT!"

"Your gangster friends got me! YOU MORON!" he screamed.

A chill ran down my back. Shawn? Was he looking for me?

"HURRY UP!" Lasso screeched in impatience.

I took one look at the cockroaches scrambling all over Lasso's legs. I wanted to cry! Oh God, please! *Why cockroaches?*

I jumped off the crate and pulled Lasso up to standing position. He was heavy, and I couldn't lift him properly. I had to bend and untie the raffia string securing his ankles. I took a long time to release the knot, but I couldn't get it off completely.

When I felt a cockroach getting into my trousers and crawling up my leg, I screamed!

Lasso screamed right back and threw himself at me. Both of us collapsed in the dumpster, his body heaped on top of mine. The filthy scary things were running all over my back now! I hurled Lasso off me and jumped right up.

I got back onto the crate, and with almost superhuman strength, I dragged him up, pushed him and threw him over the edge. He landed on the ground with a loud thud and screamed "F*** YOU!" loudly.

With a sense of urgency that I had never known before, I then propelled myself over the edge of the dumpster. I fell on the ground, but got up quickly and ran to a clearing. Like a lunatic, I scrambled to take off my shirt. My trousers followed next. I even wanted to strip off my underwear, but I checked and couldn't find anything inside.

I looked at the vermin scuttling out of my shirt and trousers and shuddered uncontrollably. And it wasn't from being bare-chested. It was a burning thirty-five degrees Celsius that afternoon!

Finally, I recovered. I calmed down and walked over to Lasso. I untied the last raffia binding his wrists. He was looking at me solemnly. Then he opened his mouth and started laughing. He laughed so hard that tears were rolling down his eyes. I glared at him, fists all bunched up. I wanted to HIT him so badly!

When he finally stopped laughing, I looked around and saw a brick. I picked it up and very calmly slammed it hard into his chest. He screeched, "OUCH! F***! YOU TRYING TO KILL ME?"

I looked at him and said coolly, "No, just the cockroach."

Lasso cringed when he looked down at his shirt. Right in the middle of his chest, a hideously spectacular blob of brown cockroach remains sat like a badge of honour. What satisfaction!

I walked away and picked up my shirt and trousers. I flicked them as hard as I could, just to make sure nothing remained stuck on the inside. I put on my trousers and picked up my bike. I stuffed the shirt into my bag. No way was I going to put that on. As I left in the scorching heat, the phoenix tattoo on my back felt like it was withering.

I heard Lasso scream after me. "You owe me big time! I took the fall for you!"

I shuddered when I thought of how much satisfaction Shawn would have derived if he had caught me instead and thrown me inside the roach-infested dumpster.

I yelled over my shoulder, "We're even! I killed the bloody cockroach!"

All the way home, I was debating if I should shave my head. Vanity triumphed. I didn't think Ariel would like me with a shining top.

24
How to Lie to Your Mum

Mum suspected I had been up to no good. She caught me soaking my uniform in bleach and using hot water to rinse it out. She asked if I had gotten into a fight. I said no, but she didn't believe me.

She left me alone only after she had checked the clothes to make sure there were no blood stains.

During dinner, I made sure I kept my eyes on her the entire time. I listened politely when she talked about the rising price of meat. I even laughed when she said she wanted to turn vegetarian. But I think I overdid it, because she looked at me suspiciously.

"You seem in a good mood today." *Dangerous ground, beware the subtext.*

"Yeah. I scored a few times during basketball practice," I treaded carefully.

"How're the boys treating you?" she asked. *Don't tell the truth!*

"They think my best friend is adorable." *Divert the focus!*

"The fat boy you told me about?" *Yeah! Got her off my back. She's thinking about Lasso!*

"You said he loves watching plays," she smiled.

I nodded smugly. "Only when his girlfriend is acting!" *On safe ground, hit her in a soft spot!*

"Shakespeare?" she asked.

"Hans Christian Andersen. *The Little Mermaid*," I replied with a grin.

"A love story!" Mum squealed excitedly.

"Relax. We're thirteen. There's no kissing on stage."

"So everyone dresses up in nineteenth-century costumes?" Mum probed again. *Where is this heading?*

"Yeah. Except the mermaid. She wears a fish tail and a wonderbra!"

Mum laughed out loud. Her eyes lit up and creased prettily. I looked at her and laughed along with her. Then a look that I knew very well came over her face. She would always slip into moments like this, thinking that I wouldn't guess.

"I used to act in school plays," she said wistfully.

Mum must have been really talented when she was younger. She used to be a lead actress in performances put up by The Thomason Players. Yes. She was an old girl of the sister school at Thomas S.R. Institute. That's partly the reason why I had to get in, too. I have to complete something she couldn't finish. She never finished college, as she had left school to have a baby. At seventeen. In a girls' home, disowned by her parents. She never told me much about them. Who needs fogies for grandparents, anyway?

My heart felt heavy when I thought of how much trouble I had brought her. Forced to leave school at seventeen, she couldn't get a decent-paying job after giving birth to me. Mum was bright, but university was out of the question. She had no means to support herself or a baby, let alone pay the tuition fees.

She lived in the girls' home till she was twenty-one. She finally found a job as a junior clerk, and could afford to rent a flat. When she was at work, I was looked after by kind neighbours, mostly elderly women who didn't mind opening their hearts to a single mum and a young toddler. Because I was very bright, most of my nannies really loved me. I picked up dialects – Hokkien, Cantonese and Teochew – and could speak any of these fluently. If it hadn't been for my deep-set eyes and sharp features, no one would have guessed my father was Indian.

When Mum was made secretary to the managing director of her company, life got tolerably better. We could afford modest means of luxury, like a computer and a television. But Mum remained frugal, never spending beyond her means. We continued to live in the same two-room flat I grew up in, long after all our neighbours had moved out and upgraded to five-room flats and private property.

Occasionally, my former nannies would return to visit us, and they would always bring gifts for me, commenting on how handsome I was becoming. I would roll my eyes every time they said something silly, but I would remember to thank and hug them. It was the charity of these kind women that had helped Mum get through one of the hardest periods of her life, being a single mother of a young child.

25
No Escape

Shawn finally caught up with me one afternoon. He was pissed when he saw me.

"Chindian! Playing hide-and-seek with me, huh? Did your boyfriend like being molested by cockroaches?"

For weeks, I had resorted to changing into different outfits after I left school. I even had different coloured caps for each day of the week. But it didn't help; he still managed to track me down.

One afternoon, I even came close to confessing to Coach. I was so frightened of being nabbed by Shawn that I wanted to tell all. But Edward was with Coach. My face must have spoken volumes, because he had a derisive look on his face when he brought up the topic of mischief-makers going around town creating trouble.

He then brought up sneakily that Lasso had been tied up and left in a cockroach-infested rubbish dump. Coach was alarmed and wanted to summon Lasso for questioning, but

I talked him out of it. I lied that Lasso had told me he had got himself into the dumpster as a challenge. Coach didn't pursue the matter.

But Edward knew. He whispered to me when Coach was out of earshot, "Watch it, you're next on Shawn's hit list."

So there I was, facing Shawn. I was dressed in a loud Hawaiian shirt of yellow sunflower prints on khaki, one of Mum's impulsive buys from a flea mart. Shawn only relaxed when I took out a box of cigarettes to offer him. I had planned this face-off for a long time. I had bought and carried a box of Marlboros in my bag, waiting to serve it up as a peace offering.

"Look, Shawn. My Fight Club days are over! I'm in a good school and I don't want to go back to my past ways," I said as calmly as I could without appearing too pleading.

Shawn thought hard as he puffed on the cigarette bought with *my* money!

"But I need your help," he said suddenly.

My mind raced. *What's he referring to?*

"I need you to restart the hand phone scheme."

My heart lurched. I should have guessed.

"I was only a runner myself! I wasn't the brains!" I blurted out in desperation.

Shawn took a long, hard look at me. Then he grinned and asked for the entire box of cigarettes. The jerk!

"Just one month. Four weekends, ok? I need you to teach my guys how you did it before. I'll leave you alone after that," he promised. Like I could trust him? But what choice did I have?

My face must have given me away. He added, "Don't even think of reporting me to your school principal. And don't inform the police. I know where you live!"

And just like that, he left. He was alone. But what did he have to fear? I wished I had stood up to him. I could easily have wrestled him to the ground. But I knew when I shouldn't give in to a dangerous moment that could turn bad; he could be carrying a weapon on him.

A fight wouldn't have solved the matter. I had to be smarter than him, and beat him at his game.

26
Getting to Work

There were more than seventy charities listed in the Community Chest of Singapore's set-up. The sectors classified to receive charity donations included "children with special needs", "youth-at-risk", "people with disabilities", "frail and lonely elderly" and "families in need".

It was a no-brainer to pick "children with special needs" for my purpose. Once I had identified a home, I wrote in as a student volunteer to offer my services to sell flags. I got a reply within three days, and was told of the available dates to report for "duty".

Part two of my assignment involved recruitment. But Shawn decided he would manage this. He did it through blackmail and coercion, getting runts who were upper-primary students. He also did some hustling in LAN shops, offering recruits $20 a day to make the rounds of hawker centres to collect donations.

Part three of the plan had me draw up a roster to station Shawn's men at the hawker centres so they could tail the unsuspecting flag-selling recruits. After Shawn had approved the roster, I took the lead in setting the first operation into action.

We chose East Coast Parkway as our first stop. The hawker centre fronting the beach easily attracts thousands of families and visitors every weekend. Swarmed with joggers, cyclists and teenagers meeting for barbecues, East Coast Parkway is also a favourite haunt for courting couples.

The first Saturday, I set the first pair of runts to circulate themselves among the diners. But I didn't allow any of Shawn's men to tail them. I needed the time to observe the behaviour of donors. I noticed that most people tended to donate coins rather than dollar notes. So I decided I had to do more to milk the sympathy of donors.

Overnight, I searched for pitiful and deplorable images of children who had been abused. They were so horrific I was surprised I could even find them on the Internet. I had these pictures printed and laminated. I handed them out to the second pair of runts working the Sunday shift. I gave them precise instructions to approach only tables with families.

My ploy worked. Most of the time, the mother would be shocked by the images. She wouldn't hesitate to pull out a note, either a \$2 or a \$5, from her purse. The father would disapprove of the huge amount, and would lash out at her.

Then I would step in. I would pretend to knock into their child, and bend to pick up a dollar note from the floor. I kept the amount I offered my victims at $2.

"Who dropped this?" I would ask, and in the ensuing confusion, one of Shawn's men would move in to pocket the hand phone left unattended on the table. I was sure to keep both of my hands visible to the victim, and not to acknowledge the runts or Shawn's men. I didn't want anyone to think that I knew them.

Following the success of the first weekend, when Shawn's men pocketed twenty-one hand phones, we moved on to seven different hawker centres.

I told Shawn he was getting greedy. When I participated in the ruse with the Fight Club Boys, we never took more than twelve sets in a weekend; that would work out to only five or six per day. And we never repeated the scheme at the same place.

But Shawn was adamant. He wanted to push his luck, so we struck more than once at Tiong Bahru Market and Whampoa Drive Market in the central region, Collyer Quay and Lau Pa Sat at Shenton Way, and three hawker centres in Jurong East and West. But we never used the same people in the same hawker centre twice.

On the last day of my "teaching assignment", Shawn boasted a windfall of ninety-two stolen hand phones. He was so happy he bought an entire carton of beer to celebrate with his followers. I refrained from joining them.

I waited till they were all slightly tipsy before I suggested taking a group photo to commemorate the event. These idiots even struck cute poses for me to shoot. Really, did they even realise how much trouble they were getting themselves into?

When I scrolled through the pictures I shot on my phone camera, I knew I had him in my clutches.

27
Trouble

I took Shawn at his word and assumed that he had let me off the hook. He had said that my teaching assignment was for a month.

Imagine my surprise when I read in *The New Paper* that a street corner gang had been arrested for a major hand phone theft scam. Their modus operandi as reported mirrored my scam so closely that I felt really uneasy. My sense of foreboding increased when the entire session of Secondary One students was made to report for an assembly after school.

Even though we were told to sit quietly, there were many furious low-pitched whispers going around.

I felt sick when one of the primary school runts that were involved in my scam showed up at the entrance of the assembly hall. He was with his mother. The principal brought him on stage. In front of close to 520 students, the boy was asked if he could identify any of the gang members who were involved in the hand phone theft scam reported in the papers.

I heard the boy distinctly say, "He's not Chinese." A silent hush settled over us.

Then I heard the principal announce over the mike, "Boys, those who are not Chinese, please stand."

I took a long time to decide. Finally, two Chinese boys sitting behind me shoved me rudely, prodding me to stand. I stood up, one of about sixty or so mixed-ethnicity boys who did.

I felt targeted. Then I saw Lasso, also standing. He cocked an eyebrow at me and tried to give me a reassuring nod. I felt really lousy. After the cockroach incident, I had stayed away from him out of humiliation. I was embarrassed to have him witness my insane fear of cockroaches. And I blamed Mum for that! That's definitely something I couldn't have inherited from my father!

I remember when I was young, Mum used to let me sleep in a *sarong*, a cloth-bound cradle suspended with a metal spring from the ceiling. It was designed for use by babies. But I had slept in that *sarong* right up till I was four! The only reason I had preferential baby treatment was because Mum was afraid cockroaches would attack me. She said I would be safe so long as I tucked my feet safely inside the cradle. It was a ridiculous neurosis of hers.

I grew so terrified of cockroaches that when I was too big to sleep in the *sarong*, Mum scraped and saved to buy a double bunk bed. She let me sleep on top, while she took the lower bunk. Till today, I never lie or sit on the bare floor of my flat; I'm just too scared of those filthy, scuttling cockroaches.

I was in luck that day. The boy couldn't recognise me. How could he, when I had ensured I looked different on each of those eight days I operated Shawn's hand phone scam. I was also careful to style my hair differently. And I had picked shirts that gelled with Shawn's people, wearing black, body-tight shirts that screamed "No Fear". Now, looking at us dressed in pristine white uniforms, I would be surprised if the boy had given me a second look.

Just when I thought the trouble had blown over, I heard a gasp in the audience when the boy pointed a finger at Lasso. Everyone spoke up loudly and nudged one another excitedly. Whispers turned into low jeers, and finally, Lasso was booed loudly when he was made to go on stage. The rest of us were asked to sit down.

I was terrified for Lasso. How could he possibly be implicated? Then the truth spilled out.

The primary school boy said he had witnessed Shawn and his men picking up Lasso after school.

"It's him! I saw him with them outside the school gates."

Lasso shook his head furiously, but tried his best to quell his fear when the principal threw him a stern look.

"But I'm not one of them! They only wanted money, I had none!" Lasso pleaded with the principal, grabbing the mike from his hands and speaking into it in desperation.

The principal thanked the boy and dismissed him. He left the stage with his mother.

Lasso was almost in tears when the principal turned his attention back to him. He asked if he could identify any of the gang members seated in the audience. Lasso shook his head furiously.

At that moment, something made me seek Edward out. I turned my head and found him standing watch as prefect. He saw me. The absolute look of loathing on his face made me sick. He shook his head at me pitifully. Then he looked away, effectively dismissing me.

I turned back to the front and almost wanted to stand when I saw the principal whipping out a long metre ruler. It was a wooden one and it looked menacing cast in the yellow glare of the stage lights. For no apparent reason, my mind was thrown back to Ariel. Ariel, beautiful and talented, standing in the spotlight reciting her lines so perfectly.

Then my mind wandered to Mum. If I were to stand up to admit I was the mastermind behind the hand phone scam,

I would surely be expelled from school. My butt was glued to the ground. Even if I had wanted to stand, I couldn't, as my legs were numb from the lack of blood circulation.

Lasso finally broke down in front of the principal. He wailed inconsolably and told the principal that he had been caught by Shawn's men and thrown into a dumpster. He said he was a victim of a stupid prank and nothing more.

"Please, sir, don't cane me! I beg you!"

Not one time did Lasso look in my direction. I felt so horribly guilty that I just clutched my head in my hands, palms pressed tightly over my ears. I tried my best to block out everything he was saying. I was in total despair.

After an agonising deliberation, the principal decided that he wasn't going to use the ruler on Lasso. But the damage had already been done. Lasso would never live down this humiliation of having cried in public, in front of 520 students.

I owe him immensely for his loyalty. Right there and then, I knew my revenge against Shawn would have to be swift. He deserved every bit of punishment I intended to mete out.

28
A Deflated Spirit

When Ariel texted, I knew she needed me. "There's no one here at rehearsal! I'm TERRIFIED!"

I cut school two lessons early. I didn't have permission, and I didn't give a damn. On my way to the school backyard, I was stopped by Edward. He must have sensed my urgency, because he didn't sound mean when he asked where I was going. I just said simply, "My friend needs help."

He took a good, long look at me before waving me away. A teacher was walking towards us, but Edward ran forward to distract him. I saw him stand right in front of the teacher, blocking his view of me. He placed his hand behind his back, beckoning me to hurry on. I made a run for it, scaling over the brick wall effortlessly. When I got down on the other side, I ran like there were mad dogs nipping at my heels.

I got to the rehearsal building within minutes. Thank goodness it was a short run from my school. It was 11.30 am, and the place was deserted. I entered the empty theatre as quietly as I could, my rubber shoes giving a soft squelch as I crossed the concrete floor. Then I heard it, a low sound of laughter. Giggles. Then, hush. Muffled sounds of "oooff" and then, "ssshhhh!"

I got close to the stage. I knew there was a dressing room behind the stage. The pompous-looking nineteenth-century ship stared at me. I felt vulnerable in the cold theatre. Finally, I made my way to the back. It was dark, and there were props blocking my path to the dressing room. I stepped around them gingerly.

Then I saw them. A stream of yellow light was beaming through the crack of a door that was left ajar. In the shadow I could make out the backs of two men. One had slicked-back hair; it was Shawn. The other, I assumed, was his henchman. The hair on the back of my neck stood. I felt my heart squeeze with fear. My hands were so cold and clammy that I had to put one to my mouth to bite some feeling into it.

Shawn and his crony were gawking at something in the room. They had their arms around each other, palms over their mouths, as they tried their best to stifle their giggles. I walked closer. They hadn't noticed me. Then I looked over their shoulders at what had captivated their interest.

My face blanched when I saw the naked back of Ariel, her long untied hair partially covering the tip of her buttocks.

She was heaving and tugging at her enormous mermaid tail, trying to pull it over her legs. I saw why she hadn't heard Shawn and his crony at all. She had on huge earphones, and even from a distance, I could hear the hum and beat of music emanating from them.

I walked up to the room calmly, and with controlled anger and strength, pulled the door shut. It slammed and clicked. But no stir from within. Ariel hadn't heard us. I turned around and looked into the embarrassed faces of Shawn and his crony.

"You perverts. Get the hell out of here!" I said in a dangerously quiet voice.

Shawn looked trapped with guilt. He straightened and inclined his head for the other guy to follow him. We got out of the building. I had to tell myself to calm down. I was so angry I wanted to take them down.

"How long have you been watching?" I asked finally.

Shawn now looked smug and grinned lasciviously. "Long enough." His man behind him stifled a laugh.

"I've always wondered what they wear under their tails. Now we know," Shawn taunted me cruelly.
I felt my veins pumping in my temple. I clenched my fists,

digging my nails into the palms. I didn't even feel the pain. I knew he was trying to goad me into a fight. I told myself not to fall for the trick.

"What do you want?" I asked angrily.

"I'm sure you've heard, some of my men had been caught," Shawn replied after a pause.

I nodded cautiously.

"So? You're obviously safe, you're here!" I spat out derisively.

Shawn smiled, but it didn't reach his eyes. "There's going to be a hearing. The police are going around looking for witnesses to testify."

I jerked my head impatiently. "So? I won't go to them! Is that what you want to hear?"

Shawn nodded, satisfied. "The pictures you took. I want them back."

I whipped my hand phone out of my pocket. I did a quick scroll and selected 'Delete All Contacts'. I hit 'Yes', and then tossed the hand phone furiously at Shawn. He caught it deftly and scrolled through it.

"Aawww, why did you delete all your contacts? I wouldn't mind asking the mermaid out for a date."

"Get the f*** out of my life." I knew I was near breaking point. If they didn't leave, I would have to fight them. All hell would break loose as they probably had weapons with them. And Ariel. I couldn't let anything happen to her! Could I protect her?

Shawn turned to leave, pocketing my hand phone. He took one last look at me and said chillingly, "It's pink with black polka dots. She took it off before she got into her tail."

When Ariel found me outside the building, I was down on my knees, crying uncontrollably. She was so frightened that I had to force myself to stop. What was I thinking? I was way in above my head in trouble. This was the secret society I was dealing with. They could have hurt Ariel before I got there!

I was lucky I had a hold over them. The jerks! They were really stupid if they had thought those were the only pictures I had. I had copied some of the pictures into my computer. But I couldn't possibly go to the police; this would be my second offence! Not only would I be expelled from school, but I would very likely be committed to a reformative centre. But who could I turn to for help? I had already caused Lasso so much trouble. The last thing I wanted was for Shawn to touch Ariel.

I let Ariel help me into the cool shade of the theatre. There in the dark sanctuary, I told her everything. My street corner gang association, my tattoo, my fights, the thefts, the hearing in the court, the cockroach trap Shawn rigged, and finally, how Lasso was almost caned because of me. She sat there listening quietly. Not once did she pass judgment by show of emotion.

After I was done, she just leaned forward and hugged me. I let my head fall into her chest. I felt her stroke my head gently. I cried a second time that afternoon. I was so relieved to be able to unburden myself.

Finally, I stopped. I looked up into her face. Her bright, watery eyes looked back at me solemnly. She had cried with me too. I knew right there and then that I had fallen for my best friend's girlfriend.

Ariel

After months of knowing Ayush, I finally understood him better today. I never thought I would feel this way for someone. My heart went out to him when he told me how he was drawn to street gangs because he had no siblings or close friends to turn to.

When I think of the little boy that he was, growing up without a father, I feel really sad.

My father has doted on me since young. With just me and my younger sister in the family, we have always gotten anything we want! Money has never been a problem.

I wasn't even aware that there were two men in the dressing room with me today! Oh my god! I could have been hurt! It was really stupid of me to go into the empty building alone. Dad has always warned me to be careful. I'm so glad Ayush was around today.

Now I understand why he is always moody. He has such a big chip on his shoulders! He always seems so much older than the boys around him. I guess growing up without a father does that to someone.

The only time I saw a man cry was when my mother passed away. I was only eight years old. Cancer is a really cruel killer. I was really young, but I remember my mother being sick for a long time before she died. Dad held on to me and my sister as Mum slipped away. I could feel his hot, wet tears dropping on top of my head.

I felt the same grief a second time today as Ayush poured his heart out. I'm older now, and I understand how much needs to be let out. As I gently held on to his head, I felt myself crying too. We are both orphans in a way – he, without his father; and me, without my mother. I knew right there and then that I really care for Ayush. But he must never find out. If he really likes me, he must be the one to make the first move.

29
Showdown

After school the next day, I couldn't focus on my basketball training. Coach picked on me a couple of times, yelling obscenities.

Then, my worst fear showed up. Shawn, together with a couple of his men, turned up at the basketball court. We ran through layups, three-on-three-weave drills, free throws, pick and rolls. They just stood there, watching and smirking. Coach noticed them, but he didn't say anything. During a break, I saw him approach them and told them to get lost.

Pissed, Shawn spat at the ground rudely. "We're waiting for our brother. There, that Chindian boy looking this way!"

All eyes turned to me. I blushed furiously. I shook my head vigorously. *Deny the association!*

"Sir, they're not my friends!" I shouted firmly.

Coach took a hard look at Shawn, and I heard him ask, "Why don't you play with my boys?"

Shawn looked pleased with the invitation. He consulted his men and then chose one huge hulk of a guy to partner him.

Coach must have been out of his mind! Picking two-on-two half-court? It was like David playing against Goliath! We were mere boys while these were men in their twenties and a head taller than most of us!

Looking over at us, Coach pointed to Edward and me. I gave Edward a warning look.

"Don't screw this up," I muttered under my breath when he got closer.

He gave me a scant glance and grinned wickedly, "What? Afraid they'd make you eat cockroaches?"

When the whistle blew, we got into action. Shawn played like a point guard in size, but he was really a shooting guard. Damned, I never imagined he was that good! His crony was just as fast, and boy, could he shoot. Within ten minutes, I was panting heavily. Their rebounds kept coming, and there were so many block shots and jump shots that when twenty minutes flew past, I wanted to collapse and die.

I looked across at Edward. His face was set in determination; he looked angry and raw with energy. He glanced across at me and screamed, "Don't you give up on me! We can do this!"

Somehow I managed to draw on a hidden reserve of energy. Remembering all the dirty tactics playing with the Fight Club Boys, I forced myself to continue. My chance came when I got a low post move. I turned, holding my elbow out at an angle. Shawn was forced to back up or get hit in the face. That gave me a small space to shoot a jump hook without getting it blocked.

That was the psychological score that turned the game in our favour. After that, Edward and I just kept it up with more jump shots and layups. Edward even managed one impressive dunk. When the whistle blew long and hard at the thirty-minute mark, our scores were even!

I fell to the ground, sprawled and breathing heavily. I had never been so exhausted before! I sucked in the hot afternoon air and smiled. Edward towered above me, looking down at my face. He had an arrogant but pleased smirk. I sat up and got off the ground. I offered a hand to thank him for a good match, but he rejected it.

He said, "We're not friends. I did it only for the game."

It felt like a punch in the chest; I was totally insulted. But I told myself that I would rise above this barb. I said quietly, "Fine. I was just going to say that you're the better player."

I had the absolute satisfaction of seeing his jaw drop. When I walked away, I saw Coach's angry posture as he stood up to the gangsters. I watched discreetly, worried that Shawn would give me away. I saw Coach jab a finger in Shawn's chest. He shoved hard at Shawn's man when the guy leaned in to grab his arm. Shawn intervened before they could fight. He lifted a restraining hand and gave the signal to leave the court.

Then Coach turned to me. I saw his disappointed look. He knew.

30
In Hot Soup

After I had showered and got my things together, I stepped out of the changing room and found Coach waiting for me. He signalled for me to follow him into his office. I tagged along reluctantly.

"How long have you been involved!" he barked out angrily as soon as I got into the room.

"I was with a gang for a couple of months before I got caught," I answered him in a small voice.

"Your mother knew?"

I nodded.

"How did you get off?"

"She got a good lawyer. I escaped going to a boys' home."

"Then why did you get involved again! You know you'd be expelled from school! That's it, your entire life, RUINED!"

Coach shouted at me in agitation. Boy, this was worse than facing Mum.

"This is a different gang. They had Lasso bound. I didn't know who I can trust to help me!"

"You know, I almost got killed once. For the same stupid reason." Coach turned pensive. I turned to see him fingering the long, jagged scar along the length of his left leg.

It was a long sharing as I learnt about Coach's past. He had got involved with a gang of friends in a games arcade after junior college. Before long, he was joining them in exploits starting with petty crimes like shoplifting and vandalism, then progressing to serious ones like running for loansharks, rioting and beating people up.

It was only after he was left to die following a clash with a rival gang – "chained to the back seat of a motorcycle and dragged", as he said dryly – that he realised he was throwing his life away. When he recovered from his injuries and got discharged from hospital, he decided to go back to university. He worked hard in his studies and landed a job as a physical education teacher after graduation.

He looked at me sadly as he told me the truth. "You should never have joined them. There's no way of getting yourself out. They're just going to keep coming after you."

His words sent a chill down my spine. I had hoped for someone to save me!

31
Book for Solace

That night, I couldn't sleep. I stayed up to read *Mr Humphry's Book of Love Secrets*. It was a chapter on courtship rivalry.

What Women Want

The key to winning a woman's heart is to think of ways to please her. Most women like to think that men are besotted with them. If you are able to convince her that she is your sun and moon, she will return your liking in the same measure. Start with thoughtful gestures. When approaching the elevator door or a door to a room, step ahead of her and hold it wide for her to pass. The experience is far more pleasurable when you see her smile in appreciation.

Nothing pleases a woman more than to know that her company is being sought after. If you are willing to fight with another man for the same woman, she will pick the victor, a female whim only men can wonder at.

Mulling over the paragraph, I realised that the answer was staring me in the face. I would just have to ensure that Ariel stayed safe in the set-up.

—

I borrowed Mum's hand phone to text Shawn and his men to meet me after school at a neighbourhood basketball court. The challenge? A rematch of the basketball game. This time, I picked Lasso to play with me. I attached a copy of the incriminating photo of Shawn and his men taken after the hand phone heist.

I said in my text message that I would forward it to my school principal if he failed to show up for the match. I was so proud of myself for coming up with the idea. I knew I could beat Shawn! I didn't need Edward, the snob. With Ariel around, Lasso was a walking one-hundred-and-seventy-six-pound basketball dynamite. He would kill Shawn when he learnt what Shawn did in the rehearsal room.

—

So much for being clever. I forgot to delete the photo and text message from Mum's hand phone. When she read it and realised I was having a showdown with a bunch of gangsters, she freaked out! She locked me up in the flat and took my keys before leaving for work.

But she had forgotten that I had a spare key. She had given it to me when she was renovating the flat. It was a good year when her company had given all staff members a Christmas bonus. Mum had spent it all. We got new tiles for the bathroom, replaced the kitchen cabinet doors, got a new fridge, and even this – my prized catch, a new Mac with computer games. For once, I didn't feel like I was worse off than any of my classmates.

I wanted to stay in school! Why should I be forced to leave because of my involvement with the gangsters? I regretted the petty crimes I had committed. If I could turn back the clock, I would do anything to fix my past! And if basketball was the only way I could extricate myself from Shawn's clutches, I would do it.

I used the spare key and let myself out of the flat. I would just have to make sure I got back before Mum came home from work.

32
Rematch

On the court, Lasso and I did some warm-up drills. Coach turned up, together with some boys from the team. Edward was with them. He gave me a look that said, "Loser, he's going to kill you without me." I just ignored him.

Then we heard it, a chant that went "ole...ole...ole...ole". Shawn had showed up with his men.

Shortly after, Ariel appeared. Her presence caused a stir. She was wearing a cute pair of very short shorts teamed with a black sleeveless T that rode just above her belly button. Great, just what I needed, a distraction for male testosterone! I grinned at her and mouthed, "Thank you!"

I could see Shawn ogling her. And Edward, too. I felt sick but checked my temper. I turned to Lasso. He had seen how Shawn and Edward were looking at Ariel too.

"You know, he had shown up at the drama theatre once, and he'd caught Ariel changing into her mermaid tail." I made a big show of sighing and shaking my head. Then,

I looked at Lasso's face. I almost smiled when I saw his face contort with a murderous hatred. Yes, just what we needed! Anger and revenge!

Before the match, I met Shawn in the centre and laid out my terms. "We win; I give you my photos in exchange for letting me out of the gang. And no more harassment."

Shawn thought for a while. Then he decided to up the ante.

He said, "I get to go out with *her* if I win."

We shook hands to seal the bargain. Fear gripped me for a second. *I hope I can pull this off!*

Just before we started the ball, I whispered to Lasso, "Ariel was naked!"

And that was all that was needed to galvanise Lasso. Forget the snivelling pee-dunked boy or his slobbering, grovelling act before the principal – kapoof – all that vanished! Lasso turned into a charged-up human torpedo. Once he got the ball, there was no stopping him. Dribble, shoot, pass, he drove the right side, scoring again and again. Shawn's men tried every dirty trick on the court, but Lasso kept coming at them.

Then some idiot threw a stone at Lasso! It must have been one of Shawn's men. The stone hit Lasso on the head and drew blood! I could tell Lasso was mad. He wiped the blood off his face, but he continued pounding the ball. He was an absolute terror, scoring twenty points, grabbing ten rebounds, and stealing the ball no fewer than thirteen times.

On the last layup, Shawn was right behind Lasso. I heard the curses of Shawn's men. Then Lasso came down the left baseline. Time stood still when Lasso took a flying leap. Shawn went up to block his shot, their bodies not touching. Then Lasso brought the ball down on a clean dunk right before Shawn's face! I saw his mouth wide open screaming a "F***!", and then the whistle blew. It was over. We won.

I stood panting heavily, body bent over, with my hands on my knees. It was such a thrilling game that I had forgotten that my fate rested on it! I looked up and broke into a wide smile when I saw Ariel running up to Lasso, hugging him tightly. He grinned like an idiot, a trickle of blood smeared across his forehead.

Shawn stared at them with absolute loathing. I walked up to him determinedly, and with Coach as my witness, I handed him a disk with the photos. He got my hand phone from one of his men and returned it to me.

He extended a hand to shake. I looked at it for a beat.

He said, "You lucky bastard, you always win." I just took his hand and gave it a limp shake, in honour of a good match.

"Stay out of my life," I warned.

Shawn took a moment to consider. Then I saw his eyes flicker over to Ariel. He paused on her momentarily before replying, "Sure."

He smiled, and with an arrogant swagger, left with all his men. I watched their backs fade in the distance till Coach put an arm around my shoulders. "He'll be back, never let your guard down."

I nodded. I vowed to myself that this would be the last time I got involved with the secret society.

Ariel was helping Lasso pack his things. I looked around, but couldn't see Edward or his cronies. Idiots! They didn't even have the decency to congratulate us on the win. I went up to Lasso and tapped him on the shoulder. He turned around and looked at me for a second, before enveloping me in a bear hug.

I felt all the air in my lungs being squeezed out. "Thanks, Bro. I got back at them."

I pushed him away. "Sure."

My eyes started to well up with tears. I faked a cough and shook my head. I wiped my sweaty brow and wet eyes against the edge of my shirt and barked at him, "Don't let

ANYONE put you among cockroaches AGAIN! I won't be around to SAVE you a second time!"

Lasso just laughed in reply.

Ariel looked at us fondly, and then finally, she opened her mouth. "Please come to my play, it's going up tomorrow night. I'm looking forward to my first stage kiss."

I must have reacted the same time Lasso did; our faces turned pale. A common understanding passed between us. The game wasn't over. We had a bigger enemy to eliminate.

33
A White Lie

The little mermaid can't bring herself to kill the prince. The prince catches her just before she throws herself into the sea. He gazes into her eyes and it dawns on him that this is the same beautiful creature he has dreamt about, the mermaid who had saved him from the shipwreck. He bestows a kiss gently on her mouth just before she falls from his embrace. The prince cries out as the maiden vanishes into a plume of mist, leaving a trail of sea foam in her wake.

On the way to Ariel's drama performance, I arranged to meet Lasso at Watson's. He must have just polished off a huge meal! His breath was foul with garlic odour, and he burped unpleasantly when he barked, "Urrpph. Yo, what's up?"

I shook my head in despair. What was the use of copying lines from *Mr Humphry's Book of Love Secrets* when he didn't try to apply what he had memorised? I bet he only brushed his teeth once a day (if at all!). Forget about rinsing his mouth after meals.

I approached the "Personal Hygiene" section and took my time to pick a breath spray. I finally settled on spearmint. Lasso spied me paying for it at the cashier's.

He joked, "What, bad breath?"

I gave a dramatic sigh. *Really, how clueless can you be?*

Just before I paid for the breath spray, I saw an entire row of laxatives. An idea started to form in my head. I studied them. The labels promised everything from relaxing stools to getting instant bowel removal. I recognised a medicinal-looking bottle with a print that said "Lactus Syrup". I should know the effect of that. Mum used to feed me a teaspoon of that vile saccharine potion daily. It had worked wonders; I never failed to poop once a day.

I was deciding between Lactus Syrup and Dulcolax, which said "suppository". I didn't see how I could get that into my victim, so I paid for the syrup and left with Lasso.

—

When we got to the theatre, I told Lasso I had something to attend to. I disappeared into the back of the building to make my way to the rehearsal room. I had a score to settle.

When it was time to take our seats, I passed Lasso the spearmint spray. He looked at me blankly before dissolving into a grin. "Sure, if you need encouragement to make you feel better."

He took a liberal spray with it. After he was done, he wiped the nozzle against his shirt, and handed it back to me. I pocketed it without using it. Lasso looked surprised, "Are you trying to tell me something?"

I just shrugged and directed my finger at the stage. The lights went down. A hush settled over the audience as the curtains lifted, displaying the magnificently recreated hull of a nineteenth-century ship. The lavish set was fixed with ornate wooden pieces, teamed with gilded railings that ran the full length of the ship's body. I was amazed that I hadn't been touched before by the magic of the set. Its imposing presence was only broken when Ariel was wheeled into view on a "seabed".

Everyone gasped! She looked like an ethereal immortal, with her long, black flowing hair settling over her fair shoulders. Her mermaid's tail glimmered beautifully in the yellow lights, its green and purple sequins winking coyly as she was twirled around on stage. And her bustier – that was probably a more respectable term for it – accentuated her feminine curves.

I heard Lasso's sharp intake of breath. "She's so beautiful...."
I could only nod numbly.

We got through Act 1 quickly. I felt Lasso stiffen and shift uncomfortably beside me when Edward, saved from the shipwreck, took Ariel, the human, home to his kingdom. Then the intermission came. Even before I could stand up to stretch, Lasso grabbed my arm urgently.

"Please, you have to think of something. She's going to kiss him! I will *die*...."

I looked into his pitiful puckered face. I wanted to laugh but stopped myself. I excused myself and made my way to the back of the building. I looked for a toilet. A stench led me to it.

There was only one cubicle. The sign on the door read "Both M & F". I knocked on it gently. A hoarse bark sounded from behind the closed door.

"Get lost! I'm going to be stuck for a while. Find another one!" It was Edward. And he sounded really in pain. It seemed that the Lactus Syrup had kicked in pretty fast. Its recommended dosage was two teaspoons; I had added four just to be sure.

The smell of diarrhoea was really awful. I stepped back hurriedly when I heard a huge splattering of bomb. It just kept coming. I couldn't stop grinning.

Then as I stood there thinking how much worse the torture could get, I saw a rat scuttling across the floor. It ducked under the edge of a cupboard and started scratching. The sound was so faint I almost missed it. But my experience as pet handler in kindergarten had taught me how to read rodent behaviour.

I bent my body slowly, stooping to peek under the cupboard. The rat was looking for a rough surface to file its claws and cleanse its whiskers. I could just about make out the length of its tail. I made a mental calculation and brought my hand under the cupboard. Stilling myself, I counted to three in my head. The rat saw me, but because I was holding my breath, he didn't bolt immediately.

At the count of 1, 2...and 3, I caught its tail deftly and pulled it out from under the cupboard. The rat screeched and clawed frantically in empty air. It gnashed its ugly teeth and twisted its body vigorously, trying to bite my hand. I just kept twirling it around in circles to stun it into submission. After a while, the rat seemed winded. When it stopped struggling, I brought it closer to the toilet cubicle.

I was holding the rat so close, I could count the number of whiskers on its face – four on the right cheek, one fewer on the left. Its moist, dark eyes gleamed at me. When a beam of light from the ceiling got reflected in them, the eyes turned red. Any other boy would have been afraid to touch it. But I wasn't like any other boy. I had spent a good part of my childhood cleaning out pet cages. The rodent was my best friend when no one else in class would play with me.

I stood outside the door to the cubicle. I knocked gently. Edward shouted an expletive, "F*** off!"

I said in a low voice, "Give me your trousers." It took him a moment to register that it was me.

"Ayush? Why?"

I replied casually, "I'm going to throw a rat over this door if you don't hand me your trousers."

"F*** you," he said in reply.

I swung the rat overhead and tossed it over the door. The shriek came faster than I had expected. I heard mad scrambling, more swearing, and then the door opened, slamming hard against the wall with a loud bang. Edward was holding up his trousers against his private parts.

He looked at the still rat on the ground. "Is it dead?"

I shook my head. "It's alive, and it's going to crawl over your feet."

Edward jumped onto the toilet bowl just as the rat came to. It scrambled out of the cubicle, with Edward's scream hastening its escape. I turned to see that Edward had slipped while doing his balancing act. He now had one leg stuck in the toilet bowl. I smiled.

He saw me smirking and launched the closest thing he had in his hands at me – his trousers. I grabbed them and fled. He continued shouting angrily behind me, threatening to skin me and do all sorts of unmentionable things.

I buried his trousers deep behind some stage props. He would be stuck in the toilet for a while. No one would hear him with the play resuming back on stage.

When I got back to my seat, I wasn't surprised to see Lasso's one empty. I sat in the dark. I knew exactly what would happen. Just as I had guessed, Lasso was forced to step into Edward's role. No one knew the play better than him. He had attended every single rehearsal with Ariel, and read opposite her line for line every time she rehearsed.

The only two times he was absent, I was there to take his place. Once, when he was stuck in hospital with a broken arm; the second time, when he was in hiding after the near-caning incident in school.

He looked kind of adorable dressed in Edward's spare princely suit. Near the end when the prince grabbed Ariel before she threw herself over the edge of the ship, I shut my eyes briefly.

I steeled myself to accept what I would be seeing. When I opened my eyes, I saw Lasso lean in to kiss Ariel.

The audience laughed when he struggled to kiss properly; his braces were in the way. Then he took longer than expected to end the kiss. I tensed up in the dark, and then it was over.

Ariel let herself slide down the side of the ship, the pulley attached to her back lowering her gently into the "sea". Lasso called out to her from the ship. As tears started flowing down his cheeks, I felt a sense of calm settling over me.

I had done my best as a friend. *Now we're even.*

34
A Truth Unveiled

After the play, I took the bus home and ran the last five hundred metres to my block. I made it barely in time before Mum came home. For once, I was glad she had to put in extra hours at the office. I locked myself in the bathroom and showered. I scrubbed my hand furiously over and over. I couldn't believe I had tortured the poor rat to get back at Edward. But revenge was really sweet.

Mum was waiting for me when I stepped out of the bathroom. She had a look that said, "I know you did something."

"Were you in the entire night?" she asked. I nodded meekly.

"You sneaked out, didn't you?" she pressed. "I called home and couldn't get through! And your hand phone, it was turned off."

"Really? I must have fallen asleep," I said. I walked towards the house phone. I took the receiver out of its cradle and listened to it.

"It's fine! Here, check it out," I said and offered the phone to her.

She declined and went to take her shower. I grinned, glad that I had the presence of mind to take the phone off its hook before I left for the play.

—

Ariel persuaded me to invite Mum to watch her act on the second night. It was Saturday night; Mum would have watched a DVD on her own if I weren't home.

I could see Mum was excited. She took her time to doll up. She chose a pink blouse paired with a long brown skirt. She even found a matching brown scarf to twirl around her neck.

When I walked into the theatre with Mum clinging onto my arm, I felt really proud when men, fathers of some of my classmates, turned to stare. I could tell what they were thinking; she was gorgeous! And they were probably wondering too if she was my older sister.

I saw Lasso sitting glumly in his seat. There were two empty ones beside him, for me and Mum. I took my seat, feeling gleeful. I poked him in the ribs.

"Come on, at least you can brag you kissed her first," I grinned wickedly at him. He looked like he was going to punch my face, so I decided that I was better off talking to Mum.

The play was a blast. Ariel was really into her role, this being her second performance. And Edward, he was really suave and polished! I thought he did an excellent job. At the last bit before he stopped to kiss Ariel, I saw him seeking me out. I just sat there and grinned like an idiot as he threw me a triumphant sneer. After what he had gone through yesterday, he deserved his little heroic moment.

I felt Lasso ducking low in the seat, covering his face with his hands. The kiss was very well executed. Lasso couldn't resist and had to take a timid peek. He dived back into the seat when he realised that his kiss had paled in flourish.

Edward, the rascal. Bet he had lots of practice with other girls.

Mum turned to me, rebuking, "I thought you said no kissing?

"They're older than thirteen on stage," I retorted.

After the performance, I left Mum to go to the library. There was one last thing I had to do. To return *Mr Humphry's Book of Love Secrets*. The library was open for visitors to browse. I managed to find the section where they had set up a display of the articles unearthed from the Englishman's treasure trove.

I took my time to read the posters on the wall. The teachers had done a good job painting what life was like in the nineteenth century. Everything was documented meticulously. There was a great deal to absorb – social norms, customs, school life, music and the arts, the literary scene, and sports. It seemed like Thomas S.R. Institute had clearly dominated the local sporting scene, in football, rugby, athletics, basketball and cricket.

There was a separate wall detailing the Institute's sporting achievements over the decades. I was drawn to the period of the nineties, when Mum used to study in the Institute's sister school. I glanced briefly at a blown-up picture of a cricket team in one of the displays. A caption read, "21 July 1996, *Thomasons Led by Captain Ali Khan Rule in Cricket*!" And in small print, "Ali Khan, middle row, second from left".

I stood looking at the photo, studying the faces of all the cricket players. When my eyes rested on one of the players, I froze. A feeling of unease came over me. My hands turned clammy, and I could hardly breathe. It was like I was staring at a body double!

I looked at the caption again. I did the Math. Then it hit me. I scanned the photo urgently, my finger counting the precise position of each player. There, second from left in the middle row was Ali Khan, and he looked exactly like me!

I was confused! Then I heard a gasp behind me. I turned and saw Mum. She must have come into the library to look for me. Lasso was with her. Her mouth was wide open, as she took in the scene of me with a finger poised over Ali Khan's face. *1996, the year Mum was seventeen. The same year I was born, thirteen years ago.*

Lasso didn't sense the awkward undercurrents transpiring between us. He stepped up to me and snatched *Mr Humphry's Book of Love Secrets* from under my shirt.

"I'll take this. I need help, by the looks of how fantastic Edward was." And with that, he walked off.

I faced Mum squarely. Her face said it all. She looked so horribly guilty that I knew the answer before I asked my question.

"Is he still alive?"

Mum took a long time to answer. She finally nodded her head.

All these years, she had refused to tell me about my father. I had even fooled myself into thinking that he was dead. That would explain why he never came looking for me. I thought of all the cruel taunts I had endured over the years, born without a father. I felt like I was reliving the hurt all over again, learning the truth like this!

I looked at her with twisted regret and pain deep inside. Mum came forward, stretching out her arms to touch me. I pushed her away.

Then Ariel came in. She saw my face and ran towards me.

"Ayush, are you ok?" she asked with concern. I nodded numbly. Then slowly, a feeling of hope and excitement surged through me. *My father's alive!*

I looked at Ariel, my heart swelling with a strange feeling. I smiled at her and whispered gently, "You were really great tonight. Congratulations." She looked up and returned my smile coyly.

I looked towards Mum and said nothing. I turned away rudely. I said coldly over my shoulder as I led Ariel out of the library. "Don't wait up for me; I'm staying out with my friends."

Mum just stood there, shame colouring her face.

When we got out, Lasso was waiting in front of the building. The three of us stood there, sizing one another up. Ariel finally broke the tension.

"Come on, let's paint the town red!" she yelled and jumped off the steps of the building. Then she dashed to the road, running and shrieking wildly.

I let my guard down and ran after her, shouting with relish and a new excitement.

Lasso came charging right behind me, laughing and hooting madly.

That's us, two boys and a mermaid. Nothing's going to change our destiny, unless one of us chooses to step out. But for now, I have a bigger dream to chase; I want to find my father.

END OF BOOK 1

Book 2: *The Lost Son*

The Thomas Titans basketball league comprises the best players from the top youth teams in secondary schools. These players are selected from the five "B" Division Zone champions. Once they are in the league, they get to play against the best youth teams from ASEAN countries. Who among Ayush, Lasso and Edward will make the cut? In the fight to emerge "Most Valuable Player", will Ayush give up his dream to find his father? And in acknowledging his affections for Ariel, will Ayush sacrifice his friendship with Lasso?

A Preview of *The Lost Son*

In a field located in Race Course Road, men would gather to play cricket. It was a Sunday and I was on my way home in a bus after seeing a movie. When I spied the men batting in the field, I acted on impulse. I got off the bus at the nearest stop and ran over to join them. I sat watching them play for hours till the sky got dark. I only realised who these men were when I saw the open top lorry that came to fetch them after the game. Twenty-two men crawled into its back, laughing, chatting and in high spirits. Although they were squashed like sardines in a can, these foreign workers were oblivious to the danger of riding in a lorry designed to carry containers, not humans.

On my second visit to watch these men play cricket, I wanted so badly to join them. I had changed into a grubby T-shirt after class but I was still in my school trousers. I understood the game they were playing. I had seen countless videos on YouTube! What used to be only a passing interest became an obsession after I discovered my father is alive.

After two hours of watching, one of the men waved to me in a friendly gesture. I got up eagerly and brushed the dirt off the back of my trousers. I ran over and nodded at him excitedly. He handed me his bat. I looked at it and tried to hide my surprise. It was an unwieldy piece of plywood fashioned into a crude batting plank. These men couldn't even afford a proper bat! I gripped it hard. The man showed me how to stand, feet apart, tip of the plank resting on the ground, hands touching the top of my knees.

"You speak English?" I asked. He nodded.

"Just hit the ball," he said. Right. How difficult could it be?

He signalled across the field for the ball. The bowler got into position. The guy did his run-up, stepped forward and hurled the ball straight at me. I froze when I saw it coming. Then I raised my plank and shut my eyes. I swung it hard on instinct. I heard the woosh of the ball missing my right ear by centimetres. I missed! I heard cruel shrieks of laughter and felt myself blushing furiously! I opened my eyes and looked behind me; the ball was still rolling on the ground as I threw away the plank and ran off angrily. I could hear rude howls and pitiful calls trailing me.

I was in a rage when I got home. I grabbed every computer printout I had of my father and tore them up. I gathered the shreds into a plastic bag and stuffed it hurriedly down the rubbish chute. I felt an immense sense of satisfaction when I heard the dull thud of the bag hitting the base of the chute. I hate him! It wasn't just the humiliation I had to swallow that afternoon. It was an entire life of derision that I had to face since he ran away after I was born.

Ayush, the bastard son. I'm so sick of that label. What was I thinking? I would never be able to get him to acknowledge me. He is the captain of one of India's most famous cricket leagues; I can't even hit a freaking cricket ball.